The Women of the Ark

A Voyage of Faith

Based on the biblical account of
Genesis 5 – 9
(All Bible texts used in this story are from The Message Version)
(Texts in the endnotes are from the New International Version)

by

Jean E. Holmes

Marjorie Ellsworth
1996 Rookwood Rd
Cleveland, OH 44112-1318

xulon PRESS

Copyright © 2006 by Jean E. Holmes

The Women of the Ark
by Jean E. Holmes

Printed in the United States of America

ISBN 1-60034-674-X

All rights reserved solely by the author. The author guarantees all contents are original and do not infringe upon the legal rights of any other person or work. No part of this book may be reproduced in any form without the permission of the author. The views expressed in this book are not necessarily those of the publisher.

Unless otherwise indicated, Bible quotations are taken from The Message Version. Copyright © 2003 by NavPress.

www.xulonpress.com

Dedication

To the memory of my beloved mother,
Dorothy Louise Cooley-Jasenzak,
a woman of great faith who first taught me to love the inspiring stories of the Old Testament. During my childhood, she read them to me over and over again, especially the wonderful story of Noah and the Ark.

Acknowledgements

I am indebted to those who gave so much of their valuable time to help me research and proof read this book. Without their expertise, encouragement and diligent attention, it would still be an unfinished thought. My sincerest thanks to:

> Mary Margaret Buss
> Phyllis Dolislager
> Dr. Bernice Reid
> Pastor Joe Hause
> June Hause
> Pastor Ron Arflin

And thanks also to the members of the Bible study group who listened to the reading of the manuscript and so generously offered their prayers, time, and comments.

Preface

Some four years before the writing of this book, I was privileged to attend a monodrama entitled "The Story of Mrs. Noah" as performed by professional actress and long-time friend, Mary Margaret Buss. I had seen excerpts of her portrayal of Mrs. Noah before, but this particular performance was so riveting that I was entirely captivated by both the story and the talent of the actress. During this dramatic presentation, I felt that Mary Margaret had truly **become** Mrs. Noah! I had my digital camera with me, and had received Mary Margaret's permission beforehand to photograph her on stage. Miraculously, I just caught "Mrs. Noah's" facial expression as she saw the rainbow for the very first time. The overhead lighting in the church fellowship hall was falling directly on her face, producing a warm halo of light. That split-second in time was a life-changing experience for me, for it was then that I knew that God was calling me to write the story of Mrs. Noah as surely as He had called Mary Margaret to perform her.

But who was this un-named and virtually unknown woman? To be sure, she is mentioned in the Genesis account of Noah and The Great Flood. She certainly entered the ark with her husband, their three sons and their son's wives. And we are told that she and her family also came out of the ark. Unfortunately, the Scriptures are silent about her name, faith, appearance, and personality. So, I wondered, how would I write a story based on a biblical account that includes a woman who is simply referred to as "the wife" of Noah?

The first problem, of course, was what name shall I give her? Surely I can't write an in-depth account of this beloved story and

The Women of the Ark

simply refer to her as Mrs. Noah! And this brings me to an amusing incident that happened just a few months later. I was standing in the check-out line of a small gift shop in Stowe, Vermont. I had discovered an adorable, wood-block depiction of Noah's ark with various hand-painted animals sticking their heads out of some rather modern-day looking windows. Standing in the line behind me was a young woman and her small son, a boy about six years of age.

While I was paying for my purchase, the young mother made a comment about having recently read the story of Noah to her son. I said something about Noah's wife, and added, "It's too bad that we don't know her name." The young woman nodded, but looked mystified at my concern.

Suddenly, the boy pulled on his mother's skirt. "I know her name, Momma," he said with a look of absolute certainty lighting up his sweet, young face.

"You do?" answered his mother. "What is it?"

"It's Grace," said the child.

"Grace?" answered the mother. "And how did you come up with that?"

In an innocent but determined voice the child answered, "It's right there in the Bible. It says, 'And Noah found Grace'."

Not a bad name, but hardly one that I could use. Then, a few weeks later while talking with a dear, Jewish friend, I happened to mention my predicament. She immediately gave me the answer that I had been searching for. "In the Jewish tradition, Noah's wife is referred to as Naamah,"[1] she said. "In fact, a Hebrew scholar who is an associate of mine once told me that the name, in ancient Hebrew, means The Mother of Us."

Aha, I had it! From there it was only a matter of coming up with her personality and character, and surely that would not be difficult. She **had** to be a woman of great faith and courage, for how else could she have given up so much? Noah's wife gave up her home, her way of life, her extended family members, and many of her treasured earthly possessions. She willingly entered a massive, wooden box filled with literally hundreds of wild creatures—and this for an unknown though most likely prolonged period of time. Surely this took both courage and faith.

As for Noah's three sons, they were easy to import into the storyline as we know enough about their personalities from later biblical accounts. Their wives, on the other hand, are as anonymous as Mrs. Noah. That's where my imagination had to come into play. I gave them names that sounded enough like those found in texts about the women of ancient, Middle Eastern cultures as I could. I have also tried to make their personalities as interesting and believable as possible by adding conflicts, hardships and joyful experiences. Conflict, after all, is a part and parcel of all lives, and it is essential to any story worth reading. Like Noah's wife, these young women must have had considerable faith and fortitude to endure the hardships of the deluge that engulfed the earth and destroyed all living things not safely ensconced in the ark. It is reasonable to assume that these women, like Naamah, were deeply affected by the loss of their blood kin, though, as in the case of Zolah, that loss may have also set them free. I chose to give the wives of Noah's three son's character traits and personalities that would both match and act as a counterbalance to their husband's personalities. It must be remembered that the offspring of their marriages eventually led to the various races, cultures and nationalities of all mankind, but that is another story.

Enough, then, of my ramblings! Now it's time for you, dear reader, to immerse yourself in the thrilling, heart-stopping story of The Great Flood and the family that, through God's amazing grace and saving power, managed to live through it. This then is my story, which I have entitled:

The Women of the Ark

Foreword
Ronald Arflin

In the midst of a corrupt and evil society Noah found grace in the eyes of the Lord. But God's call to build an ark involved the whole family. What kind of people were they?

This is an ancient and familiar story seen afresh through the eyes of Noah's wife. The author uses the Biblical account and her imagination to give great insight into the kind of faith and strength of character demanded of the entire family in fulfilling God's call in the most difficult of circumstances. The story comes to life as Jean gives us a view into each family member's personality with the ensuing strengths and weaknesses. They become human flesh, people like us, not just characters in a story. After reading this book you will never again read the Genesis account without thinking of Naamah, Rhema, Ophea and Zolah, the women of the ark.

Ronald Arflin, D.Min.
Former pastor and denominational executive,
now serving as the Director of Pastoral Services
for a retirement community in Delray Beach, Florida.

Contents

Dedication v
Preface ix
Forward xiii
Character List xvii
Chapter One—The Time Before 21
Chapter Two—The Caravan 29
Chapter Three—Two by Two 47
Chapter Four—Out of This Generation 63
Chapter Five—The Windows of Heaven Shall Open 75
Chapter Six—And the Water Shall Cover the Earth 89
Chapter Seven—Alone Upon the Waters 101
Chapter Eight—The Waiting Time 117
Chapter Nine—A Raven and a Dove 131
Chapter Ten—In God's Good Time 143
Chapter Eleven—I Do Set My Bow in the Clouds 153
End Notes 161
Resources & References 167
Contact Information 169
About the Author 173

The Women of the Ark
A Character List

~~~~~~~~~~~~~~~~~~~~

Noah – God's faithful servant – the builder of the ark. God rewards his great faithfulness by saving him and his entire family from the destruction of the Great Flood. A deep thinker, devoted husband and father, and constant in his belief that God will provide for all of his family's needs, Noah is devout in his relationship with God and communes with Him regularly through prayer and supplication. He despises sin, but is compassionate and desperately wishes to see his fellowmen saved from the coming destruction. This is a man of gentle nobility who remembers the stories his father had told of Adam and Eve, and he delights in recounting these stories, but he is also resolute in his understanding of the cost that must be paid for the overwhelming evil that has come upon the people of earth.

Naamah – Noah's wife – gentle of spirit, but strong in both faith and character. She is a true matriarchal figure. She is totally supportive of her husband, even when she does not fully understand what God wants of him. Naamah loves her sons and daughters-in-law unconditionally, but is acutely aware of their anxieties and shortcomings. Throughout the story, she seeks to bring out the best in the personalities of her various family members and does her utmost to foster their spiritual growth.

Japheth – Eldest son of Noah and Naamah. Tall and muscular, heavily bearded and swarthy of complexion, Japheth is a hunter and herdsman who loves the outdoors and understands the habits of the creatures of the wild. His knowledge of animals and how best to care for them is invaluable during the ark experience. Japheth is married to Rhema.

Shem – Second-born son. He is fair complexioned, slight of build, and has aquiline facial features. Shem is even-tempered and thinks carefully before taking action. He is a peace-maker, a gifted musician, and a deep thinker who enjoys scholarly pursuits. He meets Zolah in his mother's garden and immediately falls in love with her. Their marriage is a blessing to the family despite Zolah's sad background. Shem is the forerunner of the Messiah.

Ham - Youngest son – A farmer and builder, Ham is tall of stature and has a muscular build. His comely face, ready smile, and self-confidence are appealing traits. Unfortunately, they are also deceiving, for they belie a hot temper that lies just beneath the surface waiting to erupt. Ham is easily provoked to anger. He struggles with jealousy and resentfulness toward his brothers, and when provoked, he can be indifferent or hostile toward parental authority. He is married to Ophea.

Rhema – Wife of Japheth – Tall and stately, Rhema tends to be athletic and excels in physical activity. She is intelligent, imaginative and artistic. She sometimes reacts too quickly without considering the outcome of her actions, but she is also quick to ask for forgiveness. Like her husband, Rhema loves animals and is patient and gentle with them, but she is not above using them to demonstrate her ready sense of humor.

Zolah – Wife of Shem – Zolah has fine facial features with high cheek bones and hair the color of summer wheat. She has a lovely, willowy figure and a gentle disposition, but she is terribly insecure about her appearance and has low self-esteem as a result of being sexually abused during her childhood. Zolah is poetic and musical. She has a soft but clear singing voice.

Ophea – Wife of Ham. Ophea was born of good fortune, the only child of godly, but doting parents who showered her with the best that life could offer, but failed to give her the opportunity to learn self-reliance. As an adult, Ophea is a quiet, introverted person, preferring to remain in the background, but her knowledge of herbal medicine and the art of healing becomes a vital asset to the family of Noah.

Alena - Naamah's sister, a non-believer, berates Naamah's foolish allegiance to Noah and pleads with Naamah not to enter the ark. One of the lost.

Nimlore - Alena's husband, the leader of his tribe and a man renowned by the general populace for his great wisdom and religious zeal. He is one of Noah's primary antagonists. One of the lost.

Chapter One

The Time Before

*God saw that human evil was out of control.
People thought evil, imagined evil—evil, evil, evil from morning
to night. God was sorry that he had made the human race in the
first place; it broke his heart. God said, "I'll get rid of my ruined
creation, make a clean sweep: people, animals, snakes and bugs,
birds—the works. I'm sorry I made them. But Noah was different.
God liked what he saw in Noah. Genesis 6:5-8*

There it was again, the *hiss—hiss* sound of whispered voices. Naamah lifted her head from the sleeping pallet, held her breath and listened intently. Men's voices! Of that she was certain, and there were at least two, perhaps three of them. As she concentrated on the muffled sounds, she could tell that they were just outside, moving stealthily along the back wall of the house. Were they trying to get into the lambing shed? The possibility sent shivers of fear down her spine. Hadn't they done enough? Was their lust for blood so great that they would come back?

Naamah pushed herself up onto her elbows and scanned the darkened room. The fire had gone out. Only a few red embers glowed in the warming pit, but they did not produce enough light for her to clearly see anything more than a flicker of gray shadows on the earthen floor. The room was cloaked in darkness. She held her breath, hoping to hear the soft sounds of her husband's breathing, but there was nothing. She was alone. And out there in the night were men who delighted in the most despicable acts of violence.

What should she do? If she tried to creep quietly out the front door, would they see her? Perhaps she should stay as still as possible. If they were after the newborn lambs again, perhaps they would leave her alone. She prayed that her husband was somewhere nearby. In her heart, she knew this was unlikely. Still, she must make an effort to leave, for they might come in after her. It was bad enough that they were in the lambing shed.

Noah, as was his habit, often went out long before dawn. He would climb to the top of a steep, grassy knoll where he had a clear view of the eastern sky. On occasion, Naamah went with him, but she never had the fortitude to stay out under the starlight as long as he did. In her mind's eye, though, she could see him clearly. He would stand with his arms spread wide toward the heavens as he called upon God. Then he would sink to his knees and pray, sometimes for an hour or more. Noah was a devout man. He had, for many years, communed with God as one might talk with a dear friend. Naamah did not fault him for leaving her alone in the house like this, for the burdens Noah carried were growing heavier with each passing day.

Many years ago Naamah's husband had received a commission from God that boggled her mind. The Lord told Noah that he must build a great vessel—something large enough to hold those who chose to be saved from God's destroying hand, as well as a large number of animals, birds, reptiles and all manner of living creatures. Naamah had quickly realized that, unless her husband could convince others that their only chance of survival was to repent and change their ways, only he and his immediate family would find refuge in the ark.[2]

The task of building a vessel of such great size and the collecting of the vast array of living creatures that would enter it was beyond Naamah's comprehension. How was all of this to be accomplished, she wondered? But if God said it was to be done, she had no doubt that Noah would do it. How then could she possibly expect him to worry about her welfare every moment?

Yes, she understood Noah's faith and obedience, but that did not lessen the abject fear that now set her teeth to chattering and turned her muscles to water. Violence and mayhem existed everywhere. Not even here in this lovely valley were they safe.

Again she held her breath and listened intently. But now she could hear nothing. Not even the chirping of crickets or the gentle cooing of the doves that nested under the eaves of the house. The silence was far more ominous than the whispered voices that she had heard just moments ago. No stealthy footsteps. No sounds of soft breathing. The only thing she truly heard was the pulsing of blood in her ears and her own heart thumping against the walls of her chest.

Perhaps she should try to find the pine-knot torch that she'd left near the foot of her sleeping pallet. The dying embers in the warming pit might still hold enough heat to set afire the wads of kindling that she'd carefully stuffed into the top of the torch last night. But what good would a torch do if those men outside were intent on breaking into the house? She could not defend herself. Not from all of them. No longer was this a matter of simply tormenting a godly family. The crowds that came to laugh at the building of the ark and mock Noah's entreaties for repentance had grown surly and more dangerous. They were filled with hatred for the man who dared to expose and condemn their iniquitous ways.

Then she heard it again—the whispers and a soft footfall, but this time, just outside the front door. Her fear rose into a wave of nausea. Squeezing her eyes tightly shut, she clutched her shoulders protectively with her hands. She tried to pray, but only silent sobs came from her throat. Again she heard the terrified bleating of the ewes and the pitiful squealing of their newborn lambs. A vision of the events that had occurred just two nights ago streaked vividly through her mind.

That was when the horror began. Taking the time to wrap a long shawl about her shoulders and light her torch, with no thought for her own safety, she had run out into the watery light of predawn. Rounding the corner of the house as quickly as her trembling legs could carry her, she had entered the lambing shed. The flickering light of her torch revealed that two of the birthing pens had been torn open. The ewes were still there, their black eyes a well of fear, but their newborn lambs were gone.

The Women of the Ark

Confused and terrified that there might be some dangerous beast of prey close by, Naamah had reached for a stout club that stood near the doorway. Holding the club firmly above her head, she began to swing it from side to side. Nothing moved. Not even the terrified ewes or the remaining lambs. Forcing herself to walk along the dark aisle between the pens, she searched through the wavering shadows, certain that at any moment she would see the glowing, yellow eyes of some creature just waiting to pounce. But there was nothing. Whatever or whoever the predator was, the thief that had stolen her lambs, must have been well on its way by then.

In the morning, when full sunlight had chased away the last of the shadows of the night, she'd found the missing lambs. Their slashed bodies were stretched grotesquely across the top of the altar that her husband used for their obligatory sacrificial offerings to God. But unlike the quick and merciful death that Noah meted out, these poor little creatures had been made to suffer.

Naamah remembered looking into the lambs' glassy eyes and feeling hot tears pour down her cheeks. How could anyone do such a cruel and despicable thing? Why? Then she'd noticed the blood-spattered mud that had been smeared into the soft tendrils of wool on the tiny bodies. With growing horror, she saw the vile words that had been scrawled in blood on the surrounding stones. And then, as if the evil men who had defiled the Lord's holy altar had not done enough, she saw on the ground before the altar a small idol carved in wood. Hideously misshapen, she could tell that it was the body of a man with the head of a horned beast. The burned remains of several small rodents lay around its base.

Naamah felt both repulsion and pity. What hope could there possibly be for men who turned from the God of Heaven to worship wooden idols carved by their own hands? More convinced than ever that the Lord had just cause to carry out His promised destruction, Naamah felt her heart grow heavy. How, she wondered, could her husband continue to plead with such wicked men? How could God's patience be stretched any further?

Suddenly, her mind was pulled back to the present. She heard footsteps, then a scratching sound against the door. The heavy latch slowly lifted. Naamah cowered against the far wall of her home and waited for the evil to enter. The prayer that had earlier eluded her began to pour out. Pressing her hands against her face, she waited for the terrible fate that was about to be visited upon her. The wooden door creaked as it slowly opened; the sound of approaching footsteps beat upon her ears.

Torchlight suddenly filled the room. It flickered menacingly through her fingers, but still she could not bear to pull her hands away from her face. "Be merciful to me, dear Lord," she pleaded. "Save me from these evil men." Turning her face toward the wall as though to fend off the blows that she felt certain would come at any moment, she prayed more earnestly. "Dear God, if I am about to die, give me courage so that I may die with dignity."

A firm hand grasped her shoulder—the touch warm and strangely familiar. Still, she could not pry her hands away from her eyes.

"Mother?" The voice questioned, carrying a wealth of concern. "Are you all right?"

Naamah tore her hands from her face and looked up into the torch-lit eyes of Shem, her beloved, second-born son.[3] She could see his lips tremble and his dark eyes fill with a fear equal to her own.

"What has happened, Shem?" she asked, her voice quivering with relief. "What have they done now?"

"Nothing, Mother," he said. He reached out and gently touched her hands. "All is well. There is nothing to fear."

"But—but I heard whispering voices. There were men in the lambing shed. I felt certain that they had come back to kill the rest of the lambs."

Then another tall form loomed from behind the torchlight. "Japheth, is that you?"

"Yes, Mother, I'm here."

Japheth, her eldest son, stepped forward. He reached down and gently rested his hand on her trembling shoulders. Helping her rise to her feet, he said, "That was us you heard in the lambing shed, Mother. After what happened the other night, we decided to set up a watch. You mustn't worry, for we'll not allow them to carry out such a vile slaughter again. And we'll certainly not allow them to harm you!" A look of angry determination crossed his face as he saw that Naamah was trembling all over. "I mean it, Mother," he said through clenched teeth. "I give you my solemn word that nothing like that will ever happen again!"

After experiencing such long moments of terror, the relief that filled Naamah was almost more than she could bear. Her knees felt weak and her hands trembled. Resting her head upon Japheth's broad chest, she heaved a great sigh. "I was ready," she said, her voice barely rising above a whisper.

Shem put his hand to his forehead and gave his mother a confused look. "Ready? Ready for what?" he asked. "Do you have that fearsome club of yours somewhere nearby? Were you ready to beat us off if we turned out to be other than your loving sons?"

She looked up into Shem's strong face. "No," she whispered as she reached out and gently touched his bearded cheek. "I would take no man's life, not even if he had come to murder me in my bed."

She hesitated for a moment as she gave her sons a wry smile. "Of course, I might well have tried to fight him off. But, no, I would not knowingly wish to be the cause of anyone's death." She took a deep breath, lifted her eyes toward the flickering light on the ceiling, then added, "While I was praying, I told God that, if it was His will, I was ready to die."

"Do you not fear death?" asked Japheth in an astonished voice.

Turning to face her eldest, Naamah shook her head and gave him a soft smile. "Those who love God have no reason to fear death, Japheth. Our God is stronger than anything the Evil One can throw against us. No, it is not death that I fear most, Japheth, but rather the loss of that certain hope that God stands with those who call upon Him for deliverance."

"You are a brave woman, Mother," Japheth said. "I wish I had just a small portion of your strength. And as for Father, I'm not certain that I could ever live up to his ideals."

"Japheth, my son, your father's strength comes from his unquenchable faith in the Lord's goodness and mercy, and that faith can be yours. You only need to ask for it." She lifted her eyes toward the ceiling, then reached out and placed a hand on Japheth's shoulder as she let out another deep sigh. "And as God is my witness, we will have great need for it very, very soon."

A shiver suddenly wracked Naamah's small frame. Reaching down, she pulled the corner of her robe across her trembling shoulders, for there was a chill in the air that had nothing to do with her swirling emotions. The world was becoming a colder place. Sin was, little by little, eating away at the goodness of the earth, as well as all living things that dwelt upon it. She had come to understand this. The perfection of the Garden of Eden was no more.

Needing to feel the warmth of her sons' closeness, Naamah spread her arms wide as though to gather them to her as she had done so many times when they were little. "Stay firm in your faith, my sons," she said. "Stay firm and true to the Lord for the time grows short. I can feel it in my bones. There is a change coming. The limit of God's patience is almost at an end."

The three of them, their arms protectively entwined about each other, sank down onto the floor. And that is where Noah and their youngest son Ham found them when they entered the house. Ham rushed forward and knelt down beside his mother, for he sensed that she had just gone through some great stress.

Noah stepped forward and rested his hands in blessing upon each one of them in turn, coming last to his wife. "Naamah, my dear," he said. "There is something I must tell you. God spoke to me this morning."

Naamah looked up, trying, for her husband's sake, to keep a look of surprise upon her face. It was not easy for she had heard these same words so many times before.

"Has He, my husband?" she asked. "And what does He ask of you?"

Noah's broad smile was infectious. "He wishes me to tell you how precious you are," he answered. "And how much He loves you."

Naamah's eyes sparkled with a mischievous look. "Ah," she said. "And what of you, my husband? Am I equally precious to you?"

Noah nodded his head as he cupped her chin in his gnarled hands. "More precious than I have words to express," he said, as he leaned down and planted a kiss on her forehead.

With that, Noah rose to his full height and clapped his hands together. "Now, my brave sons," he roared, "Up with the three of you. It's a new day, and there is much work to be done!"

Japheth rolled his eyes toward the ceiling then winked at his mother as he helped her to her feet. "It's as I've said," he commented. "Neither I nor my poor aching muscles can ever live up to the expectations of this man of God." Giving Shem's curly head of hair a tug and slapping Ham soundly on the back, he strode out of the house humming a bit of a song that they often sang when they were hard at work. "Let's get busy, brothers," he called over his shoulders. "We have an ark to finish."

Naamah lifted her face toward the sunlight and clasped her hands under her chin as she whispered a prayer of thanksgiving. The chill she had felt just moments earlier was gone. Warmth flooded through her veins. The terror of the night had passed and the hope of a new day had come. Her spirits lifted as she watched her husband and sons stride out to the meadow where the massive form of the ark now rested.

Chapter Two

The Caravan

*God took one look and saw how bad it was,
everyone corrupted and corrupting—life itself corrupt to the core.
God said to Noah. "It's the end of the human race. The violence is
everywhere; I'm making a clean sweep." Genesis 6:12-13*

The tranquil beauty of the meadow was gone. Its soft blanket of sweet grasses had been trampled into dust by the tread of many feet. Mounds of felled trees lay scattered across the landscape, crushing beneath their heavy weight the last of the tender ferns and gentle wildflowers. The joyful songs of birds and the buzzing of insects had been replaced by the jarring sounds of saws and hammers biting into the hardwood trunks of the once lofty trees.

Rising from the trampled grass was the ark, its massive structure casting a dark shadow across the landscape. The exterior planking had been completed several months ago, but the waterproofing layers of pitch had not been added yet. Still awaiting was the interior work, a job that would take months if not years to complete.

Noah was not a young man when the work of building the ark began. Now, as he approached the six-hundredth year of his life, he could not help but wonder how much time was left to him. Looking back on those many years filled with hard work and diligent obedience to God, Noah knew that he had much to be thankful for. His family lineage included the lives of godly men who had enjoyed great longevity. Noah's grandfather, Methuselah, had lived for nine hundred and sixty-nine years. His father, Lamech, had lived for seven hundred and seventy-seven years. Surely, in his remaining years, he could trust God to give him the strength and fortitude to complete this great venture.

Noah was pleased with the progress that had been made over the more than one hundred years it had taken to build the ark. God had given him meticulous directions as to how the great vessel should be constructed.[4] And despite the crowds that seemed to dog his every footstep and deride his every effort, he had been consistently faithful to the Lord's commands.

Noah was also a humble man. While he had been directly involved in every aspect of the ark's construction from its very inception, it was to his three sons that he gave the most credit for the detailed workmanship on the interior of the ark. The various rooms and cages that would hold the animals were now under construction, all carefully supervised through the watchful eye of Japheth. Japheth was an experienced herdsman and hunter. He understood the ways of both the domesticated and wild creatures. He knew their habits, the kinds of food they ate, the types of habitat they were most comfortable in. Thus, he was the obvious person for the job.

Shem, Noah's studious and more technically-minded son, was busily working out the details of the bins and storage facilities for the great quantities of food that would feed the ark's inhabitants during the long months of confinement.

Most of the outer scaffolding had been temporarily taken down. The workers had used it for attaching the side planks. But the dissembled scaffolding now cluttered the ground at the base of the ark, ready to be re-used for the completion of the detail work on the interior.

Naamah heaved a great sigh as she surveyed this scene before her, for she knew in her heart that soon the peace of a sun-drenched morning would never again come to this once lovely valley where she and Noah had made their home and reared their children. Still, she was content. Somehow, over the past few years, she had come to accept the decree that God had given her husband. She knew that Noah found favor with God, thus, their family would most certainly be saved. Now if she could only stay strong in the face of the taunts that were constantly being thrown at them by the noisy crowd with hardly a moment's respite.

These early mornings were the hardest, for they had always been her special time. No matter how much work might await her, no matter how hard the chores of the coming day, Naamah loved the peacefulness of early morning. When the eastern sky turned from soft pastels to burnished gold, Naamah had the time to collect her thoughts and commune with God.

Standing silently in the doorway, Naamah tried to steel her mind from thinking about the destruction of their lovely meadow. She watched as a golden beam of sunlight played over her toes, moved across her ankles, and then crept upward to her hemline. Fascinated by the beam as it warmed her feet and then caressed the bare skin of her arms, she tried to summon the joy that a tranquil morning had once brought to her spirit.

Naamah watched in fascination as the rising sun crested the tree line that bordered the easternmost edge of the meadow. How she loved the sunlight! It was almost too much to contemplate that one day soon, she and her family would be entombed in the dark interior of the ark.

No, for the sake of her own peace of mind, she must hold on to the here and now. Another day was dawning. There was still hope. She turned her thoughts away from the ark and concentrated on the ever-changing patterns of light. She watched as the smaller pools of sunlight merged, chasing away the last shadows of night.

And as the shadows departed, the surviving fringes of the field came alive. A cloud of small birds rose from a thin line of grasses and took to the sky, their chorus of song coming to her even over the clattering sounds of the large wooden planks that were being piled together into ever-growing heaps. She turned to gaze at her fenced-in garden. She could see small insects and brightly colored butterflies flitting amidst the rows of vegetables and flowering plants. A chipmunk was busily stuffing his cheek pockets with some nuts that had fallen from her almond tree, while a brown-coated rabbit helped himself to a choice morsel of her newly sprouted greens.

Naamah felt a surge of thankfulness for these smallest of signs that the Creator of all life was still in control.

The warmth of the rising sun was a balm to the heaviness of heart that had earlier pressed down upon her spirit. She lifted her arm and pressed her hand to her forehead. If only she could muster up the same level of strength and faith that so obviously sustained her God-fearing husband, she thought, then all will be well.

Closing her eyes, Naamah lifted her face again toward the brilliant globe of light. Even through closed eyelids, she could see its splendor. The welcoming heat of it bore into her very core. Stretching out her arms as though to grasp the sun's warm rays, she wished that in some way she might store up its energy for the strength she would surely need to face whatever might lay ahead. She did not completely understand the nature of the threatening future, but she felt that, somehow, God would bring her through safely.

"Dear God," she prayed, "Give me faith to trust in Your power and goodness. Help me to understand, that whatever Your plan might be, it will be for our ultimate good."

With that simple prayer, Naamah turned and re-entered her home, ready to begin the tasks of a new day. She managed to finish her household chores earlier than usual. Pushing aside the piece of hide that covered her stores of olive oil, she began to carefully pour some of the golden liquid into the terra cotta jugs that she used for transport. Her intention was to load the vessels onto the donkey and then walk to the nearby village where she would trade her oil for several items that they didn't produce on their land.

In particular, she had her mind set on a bolt of brightly woven cloth which she had seen in one of the small trade stalls just two weeks earlier. She had run her thumb and index finger along the edges of the cloth, feeling its gossamer-like texture. The craftsmanship of the fabric was excellent. Made from the finest of threads that had been bathed in bright and durable dyes, the weaver had devised a pattern so striking that it virtually took her breath away. Naamah loved the beauty of well-made things. It was seldom that she indulged herself, but this time she simply could not resist.

Before leaving for the village, Naamah wandered out into the meadow to talk to her husband. She knew better than to leave the relative safety of their homestead without first talking to Noah. He was a good husband, respecting her enough to give her the freedom needed to be her own person, but he was still very much the head of their household. To her, his word was law, for she knew that he exercised this power with both godly wisdom and gentle compassion.

As usual, the meadow was abuzz with activity. She could see her three sons working together to cut and plane the wooden stanchions that would be used for the cages and storage facilities.[5] How many years had they been about this task of building the ark? Seventy? Eighty? Naamah had lost count. The problem, of course, was that the work of the farm still remained to be done. The demanding tasks of cultivating the land must be done, the animals needed care, the planting and harvesting completed year after year. Despite the certain threat of destruction that hung over them, Naamah knew that their everyday life must go on.

The work of building the ark, this great structure that so consumed the minds and imaginations of everyone for miles around, had now largely fallen to the hands of Noah's immediate family. One by one their friends and neighbors had turned their backs and shut their ears to Noah's earnest pleadings. Even those who had once eagerly embraced his call for repentance had now fallen away, cowed by their friends and family members, who had belittled their faith.

Year by year the crowds of scoffers had grown. "Noah's Folly", they called it, hooting with laughter when he tried to tell them of the destruction that lay ahead and earnestly entreated them to return to the worship of the One True God. "Your survival is certain," Noah preached. "If you turn from your sinful ways and accept God's mercy, you will be saved." But Noah's entreaties now seemed as ineffective as a threadbare cloak. The scoffers were only emboldened by Noah's constant pleadings, and their derisive behavior grew ever more evil and violent.

Reaching the spot where her husband sat carving out the long wooden pegs that would hold the stanchions in place, Naamah pushed back several loose strands of hair that whipped about her face in the freshening wind. She leaned down and placed a hand gently upon her husband's hunched shoulders, noting as she did the tufts of silver-gray hair that encircled the bald spot at the crown of his head. They were both growing old, Naamah reflected, but her dear husband seemed to be doing so at a far faster pace than she. Surely this rapid aging must be caused by the weight of responsibility that lay so heavily upon his shoulders. She well understood how much he loved these people who had now turned against him, but his patience with them was more than she could comprehend.

Noah looked up at her. A gentle smile crept from his broad mouth to his sparkling eyes. "Ah, wife, how goes it this morning?" he asked with a tenderness in his voice that warmed Naamah's heart.

"Well enough, husband," she answered. Bending down, she planted a kiss on his bald spot. "I'm thinking of going to the village today to trade some of the olive oil. Would you mind terribly having to prepare your own lunch?"

The smile on Noah's face faded. "Naamah," he said, "You know it is no longer safe to go into the village by yourself."

Naamah felt a jolt of deep disappointment run through her. She had set her heart on this trip. "I'll be ever so careful—and—and I won't be gone long, My Dear," she said.

There it was. Poor Noah simply could not resist the look of pleading that he saw in his wife's eyes. "Well, perhaps—but only if Ham goes with you. And you mustn't tarry there. Get what you need and return home as quickly as possible." He stood up and began to scan the field, searching for Ham.

Ham, their youngest son, was tall of stature and of muscular build. He had a comely face and a ready smile, belying the temper that lay just under the surface waiting to erupt. During his childhood years, Naamah had often worried about Ham's penchant to cast blame on his brothers for some mischievous act that all three of them had been involved in. Nor was he above snitching on them when they had chosen to leave their little brother out of their more dangerous antics. Thankfully, as Ham had matured, these behaviors had abated, though Naamah was not at all certain that they had been completely eradicated. Still, Ham was her youngest and so she had a tendency to dote upon him.

Noah raised his hand and gestured for Ham to join them. The young man dropped his ax and responded to his father's beckoning call. The jauntiness of Ham's steps spoke a great deal about his level of self-confidence. He hunkered down and placed a hand upon his mother's knees. "There's a gleam in your eyes, Mother," he said as he winked at his father. "Do you have some plans afoot that do not entirely meet with your husband's approval?" As always, his winning smile was infectious.

Noah remained serious. He told Ham of Naamah's desire to go to the village market to do some trading. There was no need to go into further detail, for Ham knew of the danger that such a trip would entail. The cocky smile left his face, replaced by the same serious expression covering his father's countenance.

"Father is right," he said, his voice now firm. "It is not safe for you to go to the village, even if you were accompanied by all three of your sons."

Naamah bowed her head and tried to hide her disappointment. Sensitive as ever to his mother's feelings, Ham reached out and grasped her hands. "Tell me what you wish to trade for, Mother, and I will get it for you. I'll take Japheth and insist that he bring along his trusty hunting bow so you will have no need to worry."

Noah placed his hands on his hips and stretched his back. He had been working for days on this particularly tedious task. He felt stiff and sore all over. "You'd better take Shem along also," he said, as he pressed his hands into the hollow of his back. "Three are better than two, for the roads are getting more dangerous with each passing day."

"Ha, a lot of good that scrawny scholar will do us!" answered Ham. Once again, Naamah could hear the bitter sounds of jealousy in Ham's voice. She gave him a reprimanding look, but said nothing.

"I'm sorry, Mother," said Ham, for he had not missed the reproach in her eyes. "But the truth is, we cannot afford to have Shem's good brains bashed in by a bunch of ignorant ruffians. Why just this morning he came up with the most brilliant idea of how we can collect drinking water and move it throughout the ark with a minimal amount of labor. Of course, he may not entirely appreciate the significance of this time-saving device as he has such little affinity to manual labor. He's too busy scrawling down lines and strange markings to be of much use with a hammer or axe. In fact, he's cost us several days' worth of labor with his insistence upon

The Women of the Ark

using the very planks that we've spent hours trying to plane smooth, for he insists that he needs them for his scribbling. Honestly, Mother, he's got them all marked up with his drawings and won't let us come anywhere near them."

Noah smiled and nodded his head. He understood Shem and was thankful for his sharp intelligence. "I think it would be well if we all rested today," he said. "We'll have more than enough heavy work tomorrow, if we are to get all of those stanchions up and into the ark." Then, flashing a knowing grin toward his wife, he stepped between Japheth and Ham and stretched his arms across their shoulders. "In fact, we don't want your brains bashed in either," he added. "I have a feeling that we'll sorely need every bit of brain power available before this great adventure is over."

Naamah shook her head in amazement, for this was exactly how Noah approached their coming trials. He saw it as an adventure—something to be looked upon, not with fear, but with certain confidence that God would see them through.

And so it was that the family was walking together toward their house when they heard the cacophony of sounds coming from beyond the ridge where Noah had planted his vineyard. They could hear the clattering of many hooves, the tinkling of bells, the braying of animals, and the strident voices of men as they labored to drive their beasts over the sharp crest of the ridge. They stopped in their tracks and listened intently, trying to make out what sort of new trouble might be coming their way.

To their amazement, several men riding elaborately decorated camels crested the hill. Sunlight glinted off the gold and silver ornaments worn about their necks. Their camels were festooned with ropes woven with vivid threads of red and gold. The loops of the ropes were decorated with bells that clanged and jangled as the animals moved forward with a slow, stately gait. Dangling between the bells were many bright, red tassels that swung back and forth in synchrony with the swaying movement of the long-legged beasts. It was a grand spectacle, one that kept Noah and his family riveted, their mouths agape and their eyes wide with wonder.

No sooner had the camels come over the hill then there followed more than twenty horsemen, and behind each horse was a line of mules tethered together with long ropes. The mules were laden with great packs so heavy that the poor creatures looked as if their backs would surely break and their ankles give way under the load. Finally, behind the last mule came a sizeable herd of cattle, driven forward by herdsman on foot and a gangly looking pack of dogs racing about and bitting at the hooves of the beleaguered cattle.

A caravan! Naamah clapped her hands over her mouth, letting out a muffled squeal of delight. She had heard of these great trains of men and pack animals that traveled for hundreds of leagues across the land, moving from one great trading center to the next. Never could she have imagined one coming to her very doorstep!

The caravan moved regally forward, its leading camels coming to a halt directly in front of the flabbergasted family. With a flick of his whip, the impressively large man who was obviously in charge of this great entourage commanded his mount to sink down into a kneeling position. Waiting for the camel to fold its back legs until its belly was flat upon the ground, the rotund merchant dismounted and stepped forward. He made a deep bow to Noah, pulled himself erect, and tipped his head to the other members of the family.

"Do I have the pleasure of meeting the man who is all the talk of this prosperous land?" he asked. Noah inclined his head in greeting. "If you are seeking the one called Noah, then you have found him," he said with great dignity.

"And are you the designer of that great monstrosity of wood we see standing in yonder meadow?" asked the corpulent leader, waving his uplifted hand in the general direction of the meadow.

Noah turned to look at the ark then swiveled back around to face his questioner. He managed to keep a friendly smile upon his face as he answered. "That wooden monstrosity, as you called it, is, in fact, an ark." He paused to see if the man understood, but received only a blank stare. "A boat, if you will," Noah added. "And no, I am not its designer, but only the humble servant of Him who has commanded that it should be built. What you see in the meadow was designed by the One True God—the Creator of all heaven and earth."

The man nodded as he stroked his thin beard with a much bejeweled hand. "Ah, yes, I have heard as much. I have been told that you claim to be on intimate speaking terms with this god of yours," said the caravan leader as he turned toward his followers and gave them a wry grin. "I do find that most interesting."

"Yes," answered Noah, "I often talk with God."

"Ah, enlightening. Yes, most enlightening. Then what they say about you is true, eh?" The merchant did not wait for Noah's reply. Instead, he turned and rudely stared at Noah's wife and sons.

"Your family, I presume?" he asked. There was a sneer in his voice that made the hairs on the back of Naamah's neck begin to prickle. Whoever this fellow was, she didn't like him. His eyes were too small and arrogant, and the line of his mouth too thin. His face reminded her of a hungry wolf she had once encountered when she'd gone out to the edge of the woods to search for berries. But this fellow was obviously not hungry. She could see the paunchy outline of his well-filled stomach pushing out the layers of rich robes which he wore.

Noah introduced his family, giving no indication that the man's supercilious tone of voice had in any way annoyed him. "Sir, it would be our pleasure to have you and your entourage stay and rest here in the shade of our almond grove. Refresh yourselves at our well, for its water is cool and sweet to the taste. And there is a stream down there in the valley where you may water your animals."

"That is most hospitable of you," answered the merchant as he shook his index finger in the air and gave Noah an ingratiating smile. "Actually, we've come some distance out of our way just to see this—this ark thing that we've heard so much about." He lifted his hand and flicked his fingers as though brushing away flies, though it was soon apparent that the gesture was a signal for one of his servants to lead his camel down to the stream. Then turning to the others in his retinue, he motioned for them to dismount.

Japheth sprang forward to help lead the camels down to the stream, for he had never seen a dromedary close up before. He was obviously fascinated with this strange animal with spindly legs, hooves the size of platters and a large hump on its back. Ham, on the other hand, stood well back away from the assembly, his face scarlet with anger, his arms folded tightly across his chest, and the cords of his neck bulging.

Naamah watched her youngest son with apprehension. There was something happening here that greatly disturbed her, but as yet, she could not put her finger exactly on it. She turned to look for Shem. He was nowhere to be seen. Feeling troubled by his sudden disappearance, she entered the front door of her home to gather the drinking vessels that their guests would need to quench their thirst.

"Mother!"

It had been said in a whisper, but Naamah had immediately recognized Shem's voice. She spun around. It took several seconds for her eyes to adjust to the dark interior of the house. When she saw him, she was startled by the look on Shem's face. He was standing in a corner with his back pressed against the wall. His hands were tightly clenched, and his mouth was pulled into a tight line.

"Shem, what is it? What's wrong, my son?"

"Did you notice the women?" Shem asked.

"The women? N—no, I saw no women in the caravan."

"They are in the back, seated on the last of the horses. There are guards around them. And Mother, their hands are shackled with ropes."

"What! Oh, my dear! No, I didn't even notice them. They must be slaves."

"I'm certain they will be sold as such," answered Shem, his rising anger turning his voice hard. "Go out and look more closely at them, Mother. See if you don't recognize them."

Naamah picked up a tray of drinking vessels, filled them with water from a nearby jug, and walked out into the yard. Slowly, she made her way toward the back of the long line of horses and mules. By now, all of the riders had dismounted. She spotted the four young women and moved cautiously toward them. They had been yanked off of their mounts and were now seated upon the ground. Six burly men stood guard over them.

One of the young women looked up. The lower portion of her face was covered with a heavy, black veil, but Naamah could see the look of fear and pleading in her eyes. Her bound hands lay in her lap, and Naamah could not help but notice that the rope bindings bit cruelly into the flesh of the girl's wrists.

With no thought for her own safety, Naamah stepped forward, trying to get a closer look. One of the guards thrust out his arms.

He carried a coiled, black whip that he held up toward Naamah in a menacing manner.

"I—I only wish to give them some water," she said as she frantically searched the perimeter for her husband and sons. Pity for these poor young women overwhelmed her. The guard reached out and pushed her roughly away.

Naamah stumbled backwards, frightened and confused by what she had seen. She ran toward the house where she found Japheth and Ham in deep conversation with Shem.

"Did you see them?" asked Shem, his voice quivering with anger, and the whites of his eyes flashing in the bright sunlight. "Did you recognize them?"

Japheth had his hand on the dagger which he carried in his belt. His fingers curled restlessly around its hilt as though he were struggling to keep the weapon in place. Ham stood beside his brother, a murderous look in his eyes and a set to his mouth that said he was also ready for action. In his hand he held a long spear, its sharp point glistening in the sunlight.

Naamah stretched out her hands, trying to calm her sons. Yes, she knew only too well who those poor women were. Three of them were the youngest daughters of parents whom she had once called friends. But it was the pleading eyes of the fourth that had filled her heart with agony. Now, looking at her angry sons, she knew she had guessed correctly. The child had barely come into womanhood when Naamah had last seen her. She must be in her late teens by now. Her name was Mesha, the youngest daughter of Naamah's own sister.

"Why?" Naamah asked as tears began to fill her eyes.

"They were sold, Mother," answered Ham. "They were sold by their own parents to these vile men to be dragged off into slavery!"

"Oh, no, surely not!" Naamah's voice caught in her throat. She felt as though the earth under her feet was spinning out of control. Her own sister would do such a thing? How could this be? Ham must be mistaken. Surely the ruffians who worked for these merchants must have crept into the village during the dark of night and kidnapped these young girls!

"Japheth, Ham, you must run to the village as fast as you can. Go to the elders and tell them that these women have been taken captive. Ask them to come out in force and help us save them."

"It won't do any good, Mother," answered Ham, shaking his head.

"They were **not** taken captive. They were sold!"

Naamah pressed her hands against her ears. "No, I don't believe it. I—I can't believe it! Alena would never allow her own daughter to be sold as a slave!" She turned to look at the girls once more, shuddering at the very thought that such a thing could happen. "Go, I tell you! Run to the village. Entreat the elders to alert the countryside to this terrible crime. Go to my sister's home and tell her to come as quickly as possible. Perhaps we can still save the girl."

When Ham did not move, she grasped his cloak and frantically yanked at it, "Please, Ham. We must help them!"

Ham shrugged his shoulders as he motioned for Japheth and Shem to follow him. They walked as though nothing was wrong until they were well out of sight of the caravan. Then, breaking into a fast trot, they headed for the village.

Naamah tried to calm herself as she went to the well to fill the water vessels. She kept her eyes averted from the men who were milling about, making light of the ark sitting high and dry on its wooden support beams. One of them turned to her and touched her shoulder. "Where does your crazy husband intend to float that thing?" he asked. "I see no rivers or lakes nearby. Why even that stream down in the valley is barely wide enough to float a single log."

The men standing around him began to snicker. They watched some of their friends stroll down into the meadow to get a closer look. It was obvious that great sport was being made of the ark and its builders. Naamah's tormentors were not about to let her go. Surrounding her, they kept up their cruel banter. "Perhaps your husband could expand this well. Get his sons to dig it out and see if the water will trickle down and fill the valley." The man guffawed loudly as he slapped his hands against his thighs. The others joined in the merriment.

The bejeweled leader of the caravan came toward the well with a small jug of wine in his hands. He smiled at Naamah, then turned

The Women of the Ark

to his men and gave them a stern look. "Listen here," he said, "This is no way to treat the wife of our generous host. Be off with you! I wish to have a word with this good woman." Naamah could hardly look into the man's eyes. His very presence repulsed her. When he spoke, his voice was like the cry of a jackal gone vicious. She could barely resist striking his sneering face.

"Your husband is a fine vintner," said the merchant with the same ingratiating voice. He pointed to the long rows of grape vines that covered the hills and then to the wine flask he held in his hand.[6] "When I asked if I might try some of his wine, he was most accommodating." Tipping back his head, the merchant raised the jug to his mouth and took a long swallow. Naamah made no effort to respond, but the he hardly seemed interested in what she might have to say.

The merchant dropped his head and let the jug hang loosely in his hand. Then, to Naamah's surprise, he offered a proposition. "I would like to trade some of our goods for a dozen or so jugs of this excellent wine," he said. Naamah watched as his eyes scanned the vineyard's storage sheds.

So this was his game! "The vineyards belong to my husband, as does the wine. If you wish to offer something in trade, you need to talk to him," she briskly answered.

The merchant threw back his head and laughed. "You expect me to deal with a fool who has let his wine addle his brain?" The heavy jowls on the merchant's face shook with merriment. "No, my dear woman, I thought it best to deal with you, for you seem like a sensible person. It is such a shame that you're isolated out here with no one but a crazy husband and his foolish sons to talk to. Of course, with the goings-on down in that meadow, by now all of your neighbors must shun you."

Naamah's mouth dropped open as she stared at the merchant in disbelief. How dare he say such things about her husband and sons! And to her very face! She felt like she was choking with the anger that rose into her throat.

Suddenly, Noah was there beside her. He reached out and placed his strong right arm across her shoulders, then gently moved her backward, away from this vile man who had come to mock and torment them. Looking straight into the merchant's eyes, Noah said, "I will gladly trade my wine for some of your—ah—goods."

"All right then," answered the merchant. "Twelve large vessels of your best wine, that's what I want. Now just give me a few minutes to pull out some of my wares." He turned and motioned for one of the mule drivers to come forward.

Noah pulled him back. "No, there's no need for that. I already know what I want."

"Do you?" The merchant looked surprised. "And how can you know such a thing before I've even shown you what I have available? Are you a seer as well as a boat builder?"

Noah stepped forward and pointed down the line of mounted riders. "I want you to release those women," he said without hesitation.

"What!" exclaimed the dumbfounded merchant. "You must be jesting."

Noah's voice became stern with warning. "It is a sin before God and man for you to have taken those women," he said. "You must release them immediately. If you insist upon trading them for my wine, so be it, but you have no right to take them away from their homes and families."

The merchant slapped his forehead and threw down his flask of wine. "WHY YOU BESOTTED OLD FOOL!" he shouted. "How do you think I got them in the first place?" He jabbed the tip of his index finger repeatedly into Noah's chest. "I paid a fair price for these women," he shouted. "Why those ignorant peasants back in that sorry excuse for a village are lucky that my caravan came this way. At least they were smart enough to realize that their daughters were worth more than the measly scraps they spend their lives scratching at the earth for." The merchant's face was fairly purple with rage.

Noah shook his head sadly. "God has placed a curse on the people of that village," he said. "As he has cursed you and all those like you. Your only hope for survival is to repent of your wicked ways and come to know God's mercy."

The merchant pressed the heel of his hand to his forehead and turned away in disgust. He walked with long strides towards his camel, but before mounting, he turned around and fixed his eyes on

Noah. "And what, old man, will this god of yours do to me if I do not—what was it you said—repent?"

"He will destroy you and all of those like you with a great flood of waters," answered Noah. "Be warned, Merchant, your time on this earth is short."

"Go back to your ark, old man," laughed the trader. "Sit yourself inside that dark monstrosity and wait for the mice and vermin to eat it away from beneath you." With a loud burst of laughter, he signaled for the caravan to move forward. Before taking his place at the head of the line, he walked his camel back to where Noah and his wife were standing. Looking down at Naamah, he shook his head in dismay, reached back and pulled a leather sack from the pack behind his saddle. He threw the sack down at Naamah's feet. "Thanks for your hospitality, my good woman," he said. "Here's a little something to brighten your days. With a crazy husband like yours, surely you need some color in your life." Then viciously kicking his heels into his mount's ribs, he rode off in a cloud of dust.

Naamah made no attempt to pick up the sack. She and Noah stood there in stunned silence. They watched as the last of the caravan disappeared over the rise. They were still standing there when their sons returned—alone.

It was Shem who approached his mother first. He bowed his head and pressed his hands in front of his face as though in prayer. "Mother," he said, "I have a difficult thing to tell you."

Naamah kept her eyes focused on the cloud of dust on the horizon. "I know, my son," she said. "There is no need to tell me. They were sold. They were sold by their own parents." It was not a question, but a statement of fact. "Alena, my own sister," she said with a heavy sadness in her voice. "What has it come to when she can sell her own child to those vile men?"

"I know," answered Shem, his eyes filling with tears. "I'm so sorry, Mother."

Naamah lifted her right hand and placed it on Shem's bowed head. "Yes, so am I," she said as the tears streamed unchecked down her cheeks. "Never mind, my son. Never mind. Surely the time for us to leave cannot be far off. For now, we can only pray for those poor young women."

Japheth stepped forward and looked down at the leather sack that lay at his mother's feet. "What is this?" he asked.

"I don't know," answered Naamah. "Nor do I care."

Reaching down to pick up the sack, Japheth loosened the cords that bound it. He thrust in his hand and pulled out the gift that the trader had left for his mother. Naamah let out a gasp and clapped her hands to her mouth. **It was the cloth—the very same cloth—that she had so desired!**

Chapter Three

Two by Two

*But I am going to establish a covenant with you:
You'll board the ship, and your sons, your wife and your sons'
wives will come on board with you. You are also to take two of
each living creature, a male and a female, on board the ship, to
preserve their lives with you: two of every species of bird,
mammal, and reptile—two of everything so as to preserve their
lives along with yours. Also get all the food you'll need
and store it up for you and them. Genesis 6:18-21*

The three women, the wives of Noah's sons, stood shoulder to shoulder in the spacious doorway peering into the ark. Light from the rising sun warmed their backs, but before them lay only dark shapes and gloomy shadows. They stood, silent, their thoughts hanging from them like baggage too heavy to carry. A thousand times or more they had walked through this doorway, but never before had they looked at the ark's interior with the same eyes as they used today. Reality—a time coming to its climax—had finally found them.

Rhema, the wife of Japheth, was, as always, the first to speak. "It is finished," she said with a simplicity that cut to the marrow.

"Oh, no, surely not yet," answered Ophea. "There—there must be something we've forgotten." In her heart she hoped that this was true, for undone chores might add a few more hours—a few more days. In her heart the wife of Ham still held doubts about the coming voyage. She had not suffered through a painful childhood as the other two had, and she was not at all certain that she was ready to take on the unknown.

Ophea was born of good fortune, the only child of doting parents, who had showered her with the best that life could offer. Theirs was a godly home, but sadly, the love they heaped upon their daughter was of such a smothering nature that she was barely able to think for herself. They lived by the principle that, if Ophea were shielded from worldly pleasures and potentially sinful friendships, she would grow to be a woman of spotless character. Thus, she went through her childhood without ever understanding what it was to enjoy life or to have a friend.

Ophea had barely turned sixteen when her father approached Noah to propose that their families be joined by a marriage contract. His daughter, he said, would make the perfect wife for any one of Noah's sons, for she had a gentle and submissive demeanor. His fondest hope was that Shem would be the chosen one.

As always, Noah gave great thought to the matter. Naamah had been certain that Zolah and Shem would make a good match, but he still harbored some misgivings. He knew that Shem needed a wife with sharp intelligence and a strong spirit. Zolah was certainly intelligent enough, but her childhood had been so filled with fear and abuse that her spirit was all but broken. Still, he felt that time and Naamah's gentle tutelage would have a positive influence upon the young woman. With these thoughts in mind, he informed Ophea's father that Shem was not the right man for Ophea.

Neither did Noah feel that Japheth was the appropriate one for such a match. He knew only too well that his eldest son's first love was the hard and demanding life of a herdsman and hunter. Japheth's powerful build and robust lifestyle would surely overwhelm a timid, reclusive woman like Ophea. The obvious choice, then, was Ham.

Fortunately, Ham was not opposed to the idea. He had met Ophea on several occasions and was pleased with her comely appearance. If she seemed lacking in self-assertiveness, surely this would not be a detriment to a fulfilling marriage. In fact, once Ham had time to mull

The Women of the Ark

over the idea, he discovered that he was actually quite pleased with his father's choice. Within the year, he and Ophea were betrothed.

Their marriage ceremony was a well-attended affair, for the parents of the bride would have it no other way. Their friends and relatives came from miles around to witness the happy couple joined in the bonds of matrimony. It never entered Ophea's head that they might also have come out of pure curiosity and the hope of seeing for themselves the massive wooden structure that her future father-in-law was constructing in his meadow.

It was likely that Ophea's parents would have chosen to heed Noah's warnings of pending destruction and stay true to their convictions, if it had not been for the sad chain of events that occurred the day after the wedding. Returning to their home in the late evening, Ophea's father and mother had surprised a band of robbers in the process of pilfering whatever they could find of value. It was never known if they had tried to chase the robbers off or had simply walked, unknowingly, into a dangerous situation. In either case, their neighbors found them the next day, lying in a pool of blood, just inside their doorway, brutally beaten and left to die.

Ophea had not witnessed this terrible scene. If she ever tried to pull the image of her murdered parents into her mind, there was no outward evidence of it. Naamah had gently given her some of the less gruesome details, but never once had anyone in Noah's family seen her mourn or shed even a single tear. There was always a bright smile pasted across Ophea's face and an airy lilt to her speech.

Thus, as the three young women stood in the doorway of the ark and Ophea seemed to voice some fear of the future, both Rhema and Zolah were greatly surprised. This was not at all the emotionless person they had come to know.

Zolah tried to soften the reality of any discomfort they might experience during the pending ordeal. "The rooms that Naamah has prepared for us are extremely comfortable," she said in a kindly voice. "There are sleeping palettes filled with soft bedding against the walls. Large basins will be available for bathing. There are oil lamps aplenty, so we shall not lack for light. I'm sure we'll be ever so comfortable, Ophea."

"Oh, yes, ever so comfortable," mocked Rhema as she let out a low snort. "Why, our husbands have even thoughtfully installed strong bars along the walls for us to grasp onto when the waters start rising and this wooden hulk begins to tremble and roll." Her voice was filled with sarcasm.

Rhema did not mean to be cruel, but Ophea's spiritless attitude often got on her nerves. Thus, when she saw a chance to kindle some tiny spark of emotion in the girl, be it positive or negative, she jumped at the chance.

Of the three women, Rhema was the bluntest and by far the most adventurous. Tall of stature and athletic in build, she dwelt confidently in her skin. She appeared to carry few doubts. Those that she did have were quickly buried beneath a thick layer of stubborn determination. She was certain, that no matter the cost, she would remain strong. It had always been her way, for she lost her parents at an early age and spent the remainder of her childhood being shuffled from one unloving relative to the other. As a result, she learned how to keep her feelings locked beneath a tough exterior.

Zolah, the youngest of the three, looked at Rhema sternly, but remained silent. Truth be known, her own thoughts were flitting about in her head like trapped birds. She'd dealt with fear through most of her life, but only since coming to the house of Mother Naamah had she learned to corner it.

One hundred and twenty years had passed since God first commanded Noah to build the ark. Each morning of those many years, the family had arisen before dawn, eaten their breakfast by lamplight, and then gone out to begin their various chores. The days had turned into months, and the months into years. Seasons had come and gone with ordered precision. Nature had followed the laws established by its Creator, and all the while the vileness of mankind had steadily increased.

Through all of those years, Noah continued to preach the message of the coming judgment and the opportunity to repent.[7] Through all of those years, God, in His mercy, stayed His hand from destroying the earth. The ground brought forth its rich harvest year after year. The rivers kept to their courses. No rain, no violent storms swept across the landscape. As in the days of Eden, the earth was watered by soft dew that rose from the ground each night, then dissipated with the first light of day. The streams and lakes remained fresh and pure, fed by the cool water of vast underground springs. People built their homes, harvested their crops, and were sustained by the riches of the earth. They lived a bountiful life, but they forgot that the God of heaven was the source of their bounty. They continued to fashion idols of wood and stone and worshipped nature instead of the Creator.

So many years, thought Zolah, yet here we remain. The ark **was** finished. It stood high and dry in the meadow where once again wild flowers bloomed in glorious profusion. Tall grasses encircled its base. Vines twined up the heavy poles that held the great structure firmly in place. Birds, wasps and bees had built their nests under its eaves. Spiders had woven webs in the roof beams while lizards and field mice found niches and hidey-holes within its vast interior. Before the journey had even begun, the ark had already become an edifice filled with life.

While constructing the ark, Noah and his sons had followed God's designs to the letter. The finest gopher wood [8] had been used within and without. Several coats of pitch had been applied to make the wood impervious to water and to seal any remaining cracks. The roof was designed to withstand the most violent of winds. The massive timbers fit tightly together, each one anchored in place with braces and strong wooden pegs. The walls had been raised to just within eighteen inches short of the roof, leaving ample space to allow for ambient light and the circulation of fresh air. This space encircled the entire ark along the uppermost portion of its walls. If necessary, the open space could be covered with pieces of waterproofed rawhide that had been first soaked in oil, then slowly dried. These shades were hung from the ceiling, close to the walls, but could be rolled up to let in the air and light. When unrolled, they were secured in place by lashings that were tightly wound around wooden pegs and hooks that had been set into the walls.[9]

The interior of the ark had taken many years of intensive labor and careful planning to complete. A wide passageway ran down the center of the long structure. On either side of this were three, sturdy floors or tiers supported by massive braces and heavy beams. On each of the three levels, a variety of compartments, rooms, cages and storage facilities had been built. Great thought and creativity had gone into planning an efficient means for feeding and watering the many creatures that the ark would house. The removal of their waste products had been a major concern, but Noah's sons had devised a series of ingenious conduits to drain off and dispose of the waste material. Many of the pens and cages had been constructed with grated or slanted floors along with a series of drainage troughs. Where necessary, special bedding materials such as sawdust, peat moss and wood shavings were to be used to absorb the liquid waste and keep down the odors.

God had given specific instructions on how each type of creature should be housed. So, too, had He given the family of Noah special insight into how to preserve and store the vast varieties of provisions that would be needed on the trying voyage. They worked long and hard to collect and prepare the foodstuff that would be needed to sustain each man, woman and beast that would be aboard the ark. All manner of grains, grasses, seeds, nuts, fruits, and berries had been dried and placed in large containers specifically designed to keep out moisture. There were vats for oil, honey, fresh water, and sweet nectars. Trays of tender grasses, herbs and other small living plants had been secured under the roof close enough to the opening at the top of the walls to allow air and light to reach them. These live plants were essential for a variety of the smaller creatures that would soon enter the ark.

Now, all that remained was this final check to see that everything had its proper place. Noah asked the three young women to make one last inspection of the food storage bins, while his sons looked over the cages where the many birds and animals would be confined.

Zolah had no idea how they were to go about collecting all of these creatures, let alone getting them into the ark. This portion of God's command seemed totally impossible. She had heard the stories of the Garden of Eden, of how gentle all of the animals had been, of how Adam and Eve had named them and lovingly cared for them. But sin had entered that tranquil paradise, and with it had come chaos. Now the animals of the fields and forests were afraid of man. Many of them were ferocious beasts that would attack and kill any poor, unwary human who happened to wander across their path. Zolah had once seen the remains of a young boy who had been torn to shreds by a pack of roving wolves. She shuddered to think of that terrible sight.

Trying to push such thoughts from her mind, Zolah entered the ark. Her companions helped to shore up one of the braces that held in place several tall containers of drinking water. The danger that any of these large, pottery vessels might, once the ark was afloat, shift and get cracked or broken was a serious concern. There would be no way to make new ones, and the loss of even a small amount of their supplies could have tragic consequences. Lending her weight to the brace so Shem could readjust its underpinnings, Zolah let a gentle smile cross her face. Despite her many worries, she was thankful to be here.

She had been with Noah's family almost from the beginning of this strange odyssey. Her father, a respected tribal elder, was once a believer of the message that Noah preached. He and Zolah's mother had always made much of the fact that they were devout worshippers of the One True God. On the surface, this seemed to be so. They went about the motions and said all the right things, but underneath all of their pious pretensions, there was a corruption so deep and pervasive that it undermined their home and all but destroyed the lives of their children. Zolah's brothers, like their father, had grown up to become men who held dark secrets. They each amassed great wealth, but did so by cheating and stealing from those who were weaker or less fortunate than they. And like their father before them, they were abusers who defiled their own children, while all the time pounding their chests and bragging to their neighbors of their piety and good works.

Zolah had lived in fear of her father from the time that she was barely old enough to understand the nature of the evil he was inflicting upon her. Eventually, she layered hatred over her fear. She ran away from home more times than she could remember, but always, her father or one of her brothers had found her and dragged her back. Zolah trembled to think what might have become of her if it hadn't been for Shem and the timely intervention of Naamah.

It happened one day when she had accompanied her family to this same lovely meadow. Noah had just begun his preaching then. His three strapping sons had come with him, each of them so handsome that they had fairly taken Zolah's breathe away. She was a willowy girl of sixteen, shy, self-conscious, and terribly afraid of men—all men. She did her best to stay hidden in the shadows, but Naamah's lovely flower garden soon enticed her out into the open. She had never seen anything quite so beautiful. Oh, yes, she had seen wildflowers aplenty, but it had never occurred to her that someone might actually plant flowers to grace and beautify their home.

Zolah stood in the midst of this bright splendor with her hands over her mouth and her eyes wide with wonder. And when she saw the translucent colors on the wings of the butterflies that were dancing erratically over the blossoms, she could no longer contain herself. A song bubbled to her lips. She made up the tune as she walked, and then added words to it. It was a song that came as naturally to her as her graceful steps. Gently reaching down, Zolah touched the petals of a flower then bent to smell of its sweet fragrance. When suddenly, a bright yellow and black butterfly flitted upward, then came to rest upon her outstretched hand; she was beside herself with joy. Her lovely song soared to the heavens, for she was blessed with a melodic voice, a gift that had, on more than one occasion, preserved her sanity. Her singing was high and lilting, first sounding like the trilling of songbirds, and then like the sound of a rippling brook. Zolah often imitated the sounds of nature, but the words were her own—words that transported her away from the frightening life that she led to some distant, imaginative landscape where only beauty and joy existed.

It was Shem who first heard the sound of singing coming from his mother's flower garden. Intrigued, he left the group of people who were standing about listening to his father's preaching. He walked quietly toward the garden. When he saw her, a girl with hair the color of summer wheat and eyes as blue as a mid-day sky, he stopped dead in his tracks. Zolah had plucked a daisy and tucked it behind one ear and was bending down to place the butterfly that had alighted upon her hand onto a broad leaf. Her voice was soft now, as though she and this butterfly were communing in a language that

The Women of the Ark

was both foreign and ethereal. Shem was not sure which of the two was more beautiful, the butterfly or the girl. He was entranced!

When he finally cleared his throat to make his presence known, Zolah leaped up and ran like a frightened doe. He ran after her, catching her just the other side of the lambing shed. Shem grabbed for her arm, wanting to say that he meant no harm, but the violent trembling of her body startled him.

"I—I did not mean—oh, child, I never intended to frighten you," he said, his words stumbling out of his mouth in a most embarrassing manner.

She only turned her face away as though expecting to be struck at any moment.

"Listen, it—it was your voice, you see. I—I've never heard anything quite so lovely before." Shem let go of her arm. "Please don't be frightened. I would never hurt you."

Zolah turned her face and gave him a wary look.

"Were you singing to that butterfly?" he asked.

A timid smile pulled at her lips. "Yes," she answered in a whisper. "And to the flowers also."

"And do they sing back to you?" he asked.

"Sometimes," Zolah answered shyly, as her eyes began to sparkle and dance. Shem looked into those eyes and was lost.

From that point on, Shem was a smitten man. His brothers would often find him sitting over his work doing nothing but daydreaming. His mouth would be wreathed in a pathetically silly smile while he sat, eyes glazed, staring into the distance.

"Ho, brother," said Ham as he slapped Japheth on the back. "Just look at this love-sick puppy. I'd say that it's time Father got the marriage bonds posted or this poor fellow will be skipping about on all fours and nibbling flower petals."

And so, as was the custom, Noah went to Zolah's father to request that Shem might court his only daughter. It was not, at first, something that Noah turned to with great enthusiasm, for he had quickly seen through the sham of piety that this man presented. Above all, he wanted to be certain that God would approve of such a match. Noah prayed long and hard about the matter. To his surprise, he soon came to the realization that this would indeed be a God-ordained union.

Naamah, on the other hand, held no reluctance. From the start she had seen the fear in Zolah's eyes, but her heart allowed her to look much deeper. Somehow she sensed that this fragile child, forced before her time to be a woman, would respond to the true love that Shem felt for her. She saw the beauty of character hidden behind the frightened eyes. Naamah had heard Zolah's singing and felt that an angel of God had surely come to share with them a small bit of the beauty that existed in the courts of heaven. But she also understood that Zolah's singing, the words she used and the tunes she set them to, were as healing to the girl as her own flower garden was to her.

And so it was that a marriage contract had been arranged with Noah offering a sizeable dowry. Later, when he had joined the many scoffers, Zolah's calculating father managed to turn even the dowry into something obscene by accusing Shem of seducing and defiling his daughter. He let it be known that the silver and gold given to him had not been a dowry at all, but the required "bride-price" [10] for the untimely loss of Zolah's virginity. Thus, not only did he besmirch the holy bonds of matrimony, but the integrity of Shem and his daughter as well.

What terrible sins, Zolah wondered, had she committed that God should seek to punish her in this way? She knew that she was comely to look upon, but was this a sin? On those occasions when she had tried to talk to her mother about her fears, she had received only a sharp word and a hard look. The frightening realization that her mother despised her had gradually dawned upon Zolah. Surely the sharp words and angry looks implied that she was somehow guilty of flaunting her beauty to entice the attentions of her father. Even now, surrounded by the love and warmth that was so much a part of Noah's family, she could not shake the feeling that she carried some unforgivable guilt.

Thinking of these things as she walked down the center aisle of the ark, Zolah did not notice that her mother-in-law was standing in the shadows watching her. It wasn't until Naamah reached out to touch her shoulder that Zolah realized that her pain must lay across her face like a smothering veil.

"The time will come," said Naamah, gently, "when your pain and hatred will be washed away. I promise you this, my child. God knows the heaviness of your heart and the pain you bear. He weeps with you. But the time will come when your heartache will end, and that which you now fear will be blown away like the airborne seeds of a thistle."

Lifting herself up on tiptoe, Naamah planted a soft kiss on Zolah's cheek, then wrapped her arms about the younger woman's trembling shoulders. They stood this way for a few moments, rejoicing in the relationship that had become so precious to both of them. Finally, Naamah stepped back and cupped a hand over her eyes, for a single shaft of warm sunlight had found them. "Now look at that," she said, pointing to a cage just above their heads on the second level. A tiny wren was perched on top of the cage, its head tilted to one side, and its bright, black eyes peering down at them. "I think that little fellow wants to make certain that he's one of the chosen few who will take this journey with us."

Zolah could not help but laugh when she saw the tiny creature. Her laughter was like a spark that set the little bird to singing, his high-pitched trill sounding both sweet and brave. Despite the gloomy darkness that engulfed him, this fragile creature seemed to sense that the great ark and even the cage he sat upon was a place of safety.

Suddenly, the expression on Naamah's face changed. She turned her head to one side and closed her eyes, concentrating on what she was hearing. "Listen," she said, placing a finger to her mouth. Spinning about, she called for the others to join her. "Do you hear it?" she shouted.

"Hear what?" Ophea asked, putting down the bucket she carried. Her pretty face was smudged with pitch and her skirts were covered with bits of sawdust.

"Quickly," Naamah called as she ran towards the open door of the ark. "There's a strange wind blowing from the east. Something is happening. HURRY — WE MUST HURRY!" she yelled as she ran.

The family stood in the doorway and looked down at the crowd of people gathered about the base of the ark. As usual, they were taking great pleasure in poking fun at Noah as he hauled a heavy sack of feed up the wide ramp.

"Husband," she called. "Do you hear it?" Her voice was laced with concern for the very air around them seemed to be trembling.

Noah stopped in his tracks, raised his hands above his eyes, and peered into the distance. By now, even the scoffers had stopped to listen, for there was a sound coming toward them never before heard. It was a deep rumbling that grew in intensity with each passing minute. A vast bank of yellow clouds had billowed up along the far, eastern horizon. The clouds seemed to roll over themselves, twisting and turning high into the blue canopy of the sky. They grew larger and more menacing as they rushed forward, obliterating the sunlight with an eerie pall of thick, yellow dust.

Noah ran down to the foot of the ramp, as he frantically motioned for his family to follow him. "COME DOWN!" he called to them. "COME DOWN QUICKLY!" They ran as fast as they could, following Noah as he hurried toward the hill that bordered the southern edge of the meadow. The crowd once milling about the base of the ark began to move back for an unnamed fear had finally gripped them. Never before had they heard such a sound! Never before had they seen the sun so entirely obscured by clouds in broad daylight!

Noah and his family made their way to the crest of the hill. They could still see the great, yellow cloud moving toward them, but now there seemed to be something at its base — a huge mass of fast-moving objects that they could not yet identify. An unearthly sound was coming from the moving mass, a mixture of bellowing, trumpeting and deep-throated calls that sent shivers up the spines of all those who watched. The ground under their feet began to tremble and shake. The tops of the trees in the forest behind them began to sway back and forth as though the very earth under their roots was giving way.

Closer and closer the moving mass came. Now even the boldest of the hecklers were cowering. Some of them tried to call out to Noah to ask him what he saw, but their voices were swallowed up in the ever-increasing roar that was moving toward them.

Several of the women who had, just moments before, been taunting Noah with their shrill voices, now fell to the ground in fear. They wailed and cried as they pulled their cloaks over their heads. But most of the crowd, despite their growing dismay, just stood there as though rooted to the spot. Suddenly, their mouths dropped open and their eyes grew wide in amazement for the cause of all this turmoil became obvious. The great moving mass was made up of animals—hundreds upon hundreds of animals—wild beasts of all kinds, each moving in perfect order as though herded by some great, unseen Hand.

Two by two they came, male and female: long-necked giraffes, graceful gazelles, massive elephants, sleek-eyed cats, lumbering bears, black and white stripped zebras. Someone in the crowd of on-lookers let out a shrill scream, as two-by-two, a great host of reptiles slithered past. Walking fearlessly among the larger beasts were many small creatures: squirrels and rodents, rabbits and raccoons, moles and opossums. A pair of long-tailed weasels walked calmly beside two tiny chipmunks, the fear of the prey for the predator now apparently gone. A male and female lion moved regally behind a buck deer and his gentle-eyed doe. Several species of bats flew over the heads of two, thick-skinned rhinoceros, while a pair of lemurs hopped along next to a variety of monkeys.

Never before in the history of the world had such a sight been seen! The crowd of on-lookers grew ever larger as word began to spread of the amazing phenomenon taking place in Noah's meadow. Some who watched began to wonder. Had this crazy old man been right all along? Perhaps it was so, for now all of these animals were walking straight up the ramp into the ark as Noah and his family rushed down the hill and ran up the ramp just ahead of the great mass of moving creatures.

"What are they doing?" shouted a dark-haired youth.

Several of the more adventurous men pushed their way through the mulling throng of animals, for it seemed to them that even the most fearsome of these wild creatures must be in some sort of a trance that rendered them harmless. "THIS FELLOW NOAH IS A MAGICIAN!" they shouted back to the waiting crowd. "HE'S CAST A SPELL OVER THESE POOR CREATURES SO HE CAN ENTRAP THEM IN THIS FEARSOME THING HE'S BUILT. WHY LOOK, THE PLACE IS FULL OF PENS AND CAGES!"

"I KNEW IT!" shouted a woman from the back of the crowd. "I KNEW IT! DIDN'T I TELL YOU TO STAY AWAY FROM HIM? HE'S A SORCERER—AN EVIL SORCERER—AND THAT WIFE OF HIS IS A BEDEVILED WITCH!"

The Women of the Ark

At this, the crowd surged backward, but soon their collective curiosity got the better of them. "What are they doing in there now?" called another woman to the three men who were still perched on the upper edge of the ramp.

"They're leading those poor, dumb creatures into the cages," the men shouted back. He tried to move closer to the doorway, but before he could step over the threshold, a bull elephant wrapped its long trunk around the hapless fellow and sent him rolling backward down the ramp.

With this, the mood of the crowd changed again. Ribald laughter broke out and began to spread. "Ho, there, Noah. Come out so we can see you. This is quite a show you're putting on for us!"

Inside the ark, Noah and his family members were far too busy to pay attention to the hecklers. They moved from cage to cage and pen to pen as quickly as they could, securing the gates as the many pairs of animals moved quietly into their assigned places. They needed no shoving or prodding, for they were responding docilely to the commands of their Creator and a host of His heavenly angels. Order abounded, and the animals showed no fear. They settled down onto the floors of their cages and waited, making no attempt to escape, as each door was carefully shut and secured by the sons and daughter-in-laws of Noah.

A calm descended upon every living creature inside the ark, but outside, the hecklers had started up again.

Zolah sank down onto the floor and rested her head against a wooden beam. "Father Noah," she asked, "are they as stupid as they are blind? Didn't they see this vast array of wild creatures coming into the ark? Could they not understand that the message of warning you have preached all of these years is coming true before their very eyes?"

Noah reached out and placed his hand on the top of her head. "Oh, my dear child," he said. "How I wish that I could have convinced them, but I fear that it is now too late. They have hardened their hearts, you see, and have closed their minds, so they can no longer hear God's spirit call out to them. They are lost, and they do not know it. They are without hope, and still they mock the God who would have willingly saved them."

The Women of the Ark

All was quiet for some time. Those who delighted in their own mocking laughter seemed to have settled down as though awaiting the menagerie in the ark to suddenly go wild and try to break out of their cages. Some of them had brought their noon meals and flasks of wine to refresh themselves. They spread their food upon the soft grasses of the meadow and talked in low voices of the strange sights they had seen this day.

And then, quite suddenly, the air again began to change. At first it seemed as though the soft breezes had freshened and begun to magnify the sounds of the nearby forest. Was it the noise of the moving leaves on the tall trees that they heard? Or was it the swaying of the grasses in the field? No, this was very different—more like the rushing waters of a brook, perhaps. Or the flapping sounds made by tanned animal hides that had been hung up to dry. But the longer they listened, the more intense the sound became. It was the noise of a rushing wind, coming from every direction at once. The lounging people swiveled their heads first one way and then the other.

There were masses of flying objects in the sky, all of them moving rapidly toward the ark as though it drew them like a loadstone. The shapes of thousands of birds, their wings strongly beating at the air, came into focus. And again, they came two by two, male and female: crows and eagles, hawks and wading birds, sparrows and thrushes. Their bodies filled the sky like a thick layer of smoke; a cacophony of sound accompanied them. In mass, they flew through the open doorway of the ark.

Behind the birds came a sight so mesmerizing that even the most malicious scoffers felt their hearts skip a beat. Hundreds of brightly colored butterflies and moths of all sizes and description flitted past upon silent wings. And behind them were all manner of other flying insects, some of them too small even to be seen, but the movement of their tiny wings could be felt. It was as though the skies had opened up to pour out a selection of every flying creature.

The on-lookers were now on their feet. They stood in speechless wonder as they watched these latest arrivals enter the ark. How had Noah managed this, they wondered? Several of them stepped forward as though ready to join Noah and his family in the ark. But then, with great dignity and a certain air of authority, their tribal elders and religious leaders stood up and sternly called them back. "This man is an evil sorcerer," they intoned. "Go in there, and he will swallow you up just as he is doing with all of those poor creatures. Listen. Do you hear any noises coming from their throats? He is a necromancer of the worst order. Surely he has cast a spell upon them or turned them all to stone."

In fear, the crowd surged like dumb sheep about their leaders. Despite the tide of evil that had engulfed the world, they still placed great faith in those whom they saw as wise men, who surely knew the will of the gods. These men had spoken to them many times, soothing their fears by assuring them that their gods would not desert them. And indeed, if, as Noah preached, there did exist a creator God who ruled all of the earth, then surely He would not destroy the works of His own hands! [11]

And so it was that, other than the immediate family of Noah, not a single person who had witnessed these overpowering images chose to enter the ark while the door of mercy remained yet open.

Chapter Four

Out of This Generation

*Next God said to Noah, "Now board the ship,
you and all your family—out of everyone in this generation,
you're the righteous one. Genesis 7:1*

A wide path of soft moonlight crept across the meadow, silvering the tips of the tall grasses and accumulating in luminous puddles on the trampled ground where, earlier in the day, many creatures had passed. The confusion of sounds coming from inside the ark had finally subsided to a steady hum, for most of the birds and animals now safely enclosed in the pens and cages were in a deep, trance-like sleep. Even the fowls and cattle—the clean animals[12] that Noah and his sons had brought in seven by seven as God had commanded—were now largely silent. The only noise to be heard from inside the ark was the steady thrum of many animals breathing and shifting about, giving the illusion that the ark itself had come to life. As shafts of moonlight spilled across the massive wooden structure, the ark's beams and siding boards began to shimmer with a pearly light. Huddled around an open fire that they had built near the edge of the meadow, the family tried to enjoy the tranquility of the night that enfolded them like a warm cloak.

The women were quiet as they watched the dancing flames, for the awesome events of the day had shaken them beyond description. As the night had drawn down, they ran out of words to express what they had witnessed. The men were also silent, though occasionally they would glance up toward the ark, cock an ear to listen for a low-throated growl or a frightened cry from one of the many caged beasts then shake their heads in wonder. They were all exhausted and bone-weary, but sleep was out of the question. The work of caging and feeding the hundreds of species that now inhabited the ark had required an enormous effort. They well knew that it was only divine intervention which had given them the strength to complete the task. Even the simple act of watching all of the creatures move methodically up the ramp and in through the wide doorway was mind-numbing, a fact that was quite apparent when the stunned crowds of on-lookers began to slink away well before sunset.

Earlier in the evening, the family talked of the day's events until it seemed that there were no more words to be said. Now they were resorting to mundane tasks in an effort to relax their whirling minds. Noah and Ham absentmindedly whittled away at wooden pegs as though their hands could not cease in the making of such objects, although they already had a vast supply. Japheth was scraping the inside of a small animal hide that he stretched on a wooden frame set up near the fire pit. Shem idly played his zephyr, starting one tune, but never quite finishing it before he began another.

Naamah occupied herself with her favorite pastime, making bread. She kneaded the soft lump of dough over and over again, hardly thinking of what she was doing. Her eyes traveled from the face of one family member to the other as she sought for happy memories that would bring comfort to her heart. Each face, softened by the flickering firelight, seemed to hold an inner glow that attested to their resolve to see the coming venture through, no matter what the personal cost.

How dear these faces were, thought Naamah. Her husband's, scored by age, hard manual labor and the many years of pleading with the people he cared so much for still held the gentle nobility that she had found so attractive when she first came to him as a young bride. Next the faces of her three sons held her attention, each one so different and yet so alike, for there was a bit of both Noah and herself in them. Shem had the high forehead and the serious eyes of a scholar. Ham, the farmer and builder, held many fine lines radiating out from his eyes, giving him the look of one who had spent many hours squinting at a measuring device or checking the alignment of one thing or another. Japheth, the herdsman and hunter, his complexion so swarthy and his beard so dense that it was difficult to see any facial lines at all, was more difficult to read. Still, Naamah knew every crease and hollow by heart and loved them well, for they were a certain measure of her eldest son's gentle ways with animals and the devotion he felt for his family.

Picking up the well-kneaded lump of dough, Naamah turned it over several times then firmly slapped it down onto the wide, flat rock that she had used for bread making for more years than she could remember. The coals in her dome-shaped oven were almost ready. She could see the hot glow of them through the rounded opening that was the oven's doorway. Mesmerized by that steady glow, she let her mind drift.

Would this be the last loaf of bread she would ever bake in her own oven? She remembered the day so long ago when her dear husband had taken her by the hand and led her to this lovely meadow to show her the spot where he was building their new home. In her mind's eye, she saw again the pride in his face as he told her of his plans to plant a vineyard that would spread across the rolling hills surrounding the meadow. And she remembered the day he gathered stones and clay from the nearby stream to build her this oven. She recalled again the births of their three fine sons, their happy childhoods, and those special times when they courted and married.

Suddenly, despite the warmth coming from the oven and the nearby fire, Naamah felt a chilling shiver run down her spine. All of those wonderful years were gone, swallowed up by this impending danger. And the many years of preparation—how had she used them? Had she squandered too much time with unimportant activities or inconsequential worries? Had she ever really faced the truth of the dire warnings that God had given to her husband?

Slowly, the reality of what was about to happen dawned on her, and with reality came fear—not the nagging worries she'd entertained in the past, but an overwhelming horror that struck her with such a force that she felt she might fall face-first into her own oven. A sharp jolt of pain suddenly coursed through her hands, then travel upward into her arms and shoulders. Glancing down to determine the source of such discomfort, she realized that she was pressing down so hard onto the ball of dough that it had almost disintegrated, leaving nothing to cushion the palms of her hands from the hard surface of the stone.

"Mother, what's wrong?" Naamah turned to see Rhema staring at her.

"It—it's nothing," Naamah stammered.

"But of course it's something," said Rhema as she put down the lump of clay that she was molding into a small, fluted dish. All three of Naamah's daughter-in-laws were adept at making pottery vessels, but Rhema had a special talent for creating the loveliest pieces. After they were fired, she painted beautiful designs on them—geometric designs, pictures of birds in flight, intricately curling vines, and slender-legged animals that seemed to fairly swirl around the vessels that held them.

Rhema's remarks immediately drew the attention of Ophea and Zolah. Suddenly worried, they clustered around their mother-in-law, for they loved her dearly and were ever solicitous of her feelings and needs. Ophea had been blowing quietly into the mouthpiece of the flute that her husband Ham had lovingly fashioned for her. She was not a musician, but she played from the depths of her heart. With a little encouragement, she could play a passable tune. Now she sank down next to Naamah and placed her hands gently on the older woman's knees. "Shall I play something soothing for you, Mother?" she asked.

Naamah allowed a warm smile to creep across her face. "Yes, that would be nice," she said. "I think we all need to be calmed about now."

Ophea began to gently blow upon her flute. Soon Shem joined in on his lyre, for the melody was something he composed several weeks ago. Zolah's natural talent for poetry took up the challenge. Within minutes she composed words that told of the beauty of the earth, the warmth of sunlight, the subtle glow of moonlight, and the love of a family for all that God had created. Her high, lilting voice filtered out into the meadow. Soon the whole family took up the refrain. They sang with such joy that the sounds of their singing must surely have soothed the creatures enclosed in the ark, for even the sounds of their breathing seemed to soften.

The full moon rode high over the tree-line pulling with it the ever-changing patterns of silvery light and deep shadows. The family sensed that this would surely be their last night here in the lovely meadow that had been their home and the place where their hopes for the future were so firmly anchored. They had completed the task that God had given them. Now it was only a matter of waiting for His final command to enter the great structure that would offer them sanctuary from His promised judgment.

The pale light of morning sunshine that awakened the family to a new day was completely different from the bright glow of previous mornings. Even the air seemed to have changed. There was a heaviness that pressed on the lungs so that breathing was more difficult. Strangely, there had been no mist the night before, leaving the ground brittle and dry to the touch. The gentle breezes that, in the past, wafted across the landscape, cooling the earth and setting the leaves on the trees to rustle in a rhythmic cadence, were completely absent. It was as though the entire earth was waiting for some great change while the sky above held its breath in silent anticipation.

Occasionally, dark clouds would scud across the sky, but the wind that blew them did not touch the gathering crowd who watched uneasily from below. As usual, the people came to gawk at the ark and fling insults at Noah and his family, but now there seemed to be a growing viciousness in the way they shoved at each other, each hoping to get a glimpse of some of the wild creatures that were housed within "Noah's Monstrosity".

"Ho there, old man, have the lions eaten your wife yet? Are the leopards gnawing at the bones of your sons?"

As Noah walked past the belligerent crowd, he looked neither to the right or left. He had been out in the field praying since well before sunrise, for he sensed that the day had come at last when God would again speak to him. Just as the sun crested the eastern horizon, Noah looked up into the brightening sky and heard the commanding voice of the Lord.

The Women of the Ark

"IT IS TIME, NOAH," God said. "TAKE YOUR WIFE, YOUR SONS, AND YOUR SON'S WIVES AND ENTER THE ARK."

When Noah entered his home, he found everything in readiness. His family barely slept the night before. Now they observed by the look on his face that the time had come. They scarcely spoke a word to each other as they picked up the last of their bundles and walked resolutely toward the ramp that led to the open door of the ark. Noah led the solemn procession, but when he reached the end of the ramp, he stepped back and took Naamah's arm. "You and the young women must go first," he said. "My sons and I will wait here until you are safely inside."

Namaah nodded her head, turned one last time to look at the lovely meadow, then began to ascend the ramp. She pulled up short when she heard someone from the crowd calling her name. Turning, she looked down into the confused eyes of her sister, Alena. "Why are you doing this?" Alena asked. "Surely you will not turn your back on your entire family to obey the ravings of this lunatic? Come down and we will care for you, Naamah. You belong with your own people."

Naamah looked down at her sister with such an expression of pity that tears sprang to her eyes as well as her sister's. "These **are** my people," she said as she turned her palms inward and stretched out her arms as though to gather her husband and sons into them. "And these are my own beloved daughters," she added, as she smiled at the three, younger women standing near her on the ramp.

Then, looking up at the ark and spreading her arms wide, a brilliant smile lit up Naamah's face. "And this great vessel that we are about to enter is the house of our God. Why then should I be fearful? It is His hands that cover us, Alena, and it is His power that will lift up this ship and carry it and all of those who are within safely across the flood waters."

Suddenly, a man standing next to Alena jumped forward. It was Nimlore, Alena's husband, the leader of his tribe and a man renowned for his great wisdom. "And what has this god of yours done for you, old woman?" he asked in a rude manner. "Look about you. He has turned all of you into mindless slaves. You obey his every whim. You and your husband have given up everything that is good in life to build this monstrosity. Your god has forced you to labor day-in and day-out for more than one hundred years. You have cut down the forests that once sheltered your land. You have denuded the fields of their bounty to store their fruits and grains in this *thing* you call an ark, and are willing to sit in there and watch them all slowly rot away. You have captured the creatures of the earth and caged them up so they may no longer run free as they were meant to do. And now, Naamah—now your sister comes to you in kindness, offering to shelter you, and what do you say? You mouth the words of your deluded husband as though he himself had created the earth. BLASPHEMY, I SAY! IT IS UTTER BLASPHEMY!"

Alena stretched out her hand to Naamah. "Please, dear sister, listen to my husband, for he speaks the truth. Come down from there, and let us care for you."

Suddenly, a deranged old man, his beard caked with dried food and his scraggly hair a nest of knots and tangles, jumped forward. Grasping at Naamah's ankles, he began to cackle and crow. "Yes, my sweet, my gentle pigeon dove," he sneered. "Come down here, and we will most certainly care for you." Then, folding his dirty hands against his breast as though in earnest entreaty, the old man gave the three young women cowering behind Naamah a lecherous wink. "And your lovely daughters-in-law." he sneered. "Oh, yes, send down those goddesses of beauty, and we will teach them the pleasures of both this world and the next!"

With that, the crowd broke out into ribald laughter as they made obscene gestures towards the three young women. Alena shrank back into the crowd and disappeared.

Appalled beyond words, Naamah could only look out into the upturned faces and shake her head with incredulous sorrow. Full sunlight was upon them now, illuminating their faces in such a way that even its golden beams accentuated the hard lines of hatred. Try as she might, Naamah could not see a trace of true beauty nor the smallest amount of human compassion. It was then that she came to the realization that she was finally seeing them for what they truly were. The hardness of their eyes, the lines of hatred that marked their faces, their arrogance and pride, their love for ostentatious adornment, the pleasure that they experienced when they inflicted pain, their propensity for the worst forms of cruelty shocked her.

These were not merely human beings who lusted after evil—they were the very embodiment of it!

And now, for the very first time, Naamah knew why the heart of God was broken when He looked down and saw what had become of this human race that He had so lovingly created in His own image. She understood why the Lord saw Noah and his family as the very last hope for humanity.

The trembling in Naamah's legs worked its way up into her body. It reached her arms and then her hands. It was all she could do keep herself upright and hold onto the small sack that she carried. Seeing her mother-in-law's rising panic, Rhema grabbed her arm and began leading her up the long ramp. Ophea followed close behind. They stopped short, however, when they reached Zolah, for the frightened young woman was rooted to the spot directly in front of the doorway.

"ZOLAH!" shouted Rhema. "GET INSIDE!"

Zolah remained frozen in place.

By now, Ophea's normally placid manner had fallen to shreds. Attempting to squeeze past Rhema and her mother-in-law, she gave Zolah a hard shove. "ZOLAH!" she screamed, for it was now difficult to be heard over the shouting mob that swarmed around the base of the ramp like a nest of angry hornets. Giving her sister-in-law a head-jerking shake, she took one last look at the mob and all but pushed Zolah off the ramp in her effort to get through the doorway. "You useless fool!" she spit out. "I've had just about enough of your ridiculous hysterics. Now get out of my way!" With that, Ophea stumbled through the doorway and disappeared into the cavernous interior of the ark.

Rhema was only slightly more solicitous of Zolah's terror. "Listen, little sister," she said through gritted teeth. "We know that you suffered through an unhappy childhood and that you still carry those bad memories locked away in your heart, but this is **not** the time for second thoughts. If we don't get through this door soon, you'll think that the evils that beset your girlhood were little more than bad dreams! If those men down there get their hands on us . . ."

Rhema never got the chance to finish the sentence, for Naamah suddenly stepped between them. She gave Rhema a reprimanding shake of her head as she wrapped her arms protectively about Zolah's trembling body. "Come, child," she said, her voice gentle and filled with compassion. "Let me help you."

Still, Zolah did not move. Her face was a mask of terror. She stood as though paralyzed, her eyes fixed on the gaping doorway and the dark shadows beyond. She was like a defenseless animal caught in a fearsome trap. Her clenched fists pressed hard against her mouth as though to stifle a scream, but no sound came.

Rhema swiveled her head around to search for the men of the family. When she saw them, her heart leaped into her throat. With the angry mob almost surrounding them, Noah and his sons were desperately trying to work their way up the now crowded ramp. She could see her husband Japheth standing protectively in front of his father. He brandished a large cudgel in his right hand, and his left arm was extended outward to ward off the jabbing fists of the bolder members of the mob. Turning first one way and then the other, he looked like a formidable obstacle, but Rhema knew that it was only a matter of time before the angry mob might mow him down.

Noah and his other two sons were backing up the ramp, but they were further along than Japheth and carried nothing that could remotely be used as a weapon. Suddenly, Shem turned to see how far the women had gotten. When he saw Zolah frozen in place at the top of the ramp, his face turned ashen. Leaving his father in the care of his two brothers, Shem took the steep incline of the ramp in six long strides.

"ZOLAH!" he shouted. "What in the name of the Most Holy are you doing? Can't you see what's happening? We'll all be lost if you don't get through this doorway! NOW, ZOLAH, GET IN THERE **NOW!**"

Reaching out as though to lift her up bodily and carry her over the threshold, Shem was suddenly stopped by Naamah's outstretched hand. "Leave her be, Shem." she said with a determination that brought him up short. "Go back down there and help your father and brothers. They have far more need of you than we do."

Shem hesitated, but only for a moment, for the steely look of authority in his mother's eyes was unmistakable.

"What is it that so frightens you?" asked Naamah as she again turned her full attention on the young woman. "Surely you have nothing to fear in entering the ark. Haven't you done it hundreds of times before?"

Zolah turned her head mechanically and gave the older woman a glassy-eyed stare. "*I can't,*" she mouthed the words, for no sounds could be heard above the roar of the mob. Naamah had no need to hear the words. The second she saw Zolah's gaze go to the massive doorway, she understood.

"It's the door, isn't it?" asked Naamah. "You're afraid of what might happen when the door is closed."

"*Dark! So dark! No way out! He won't let me out!*" whispered Zolah as tears streamed down her stricken face.

Watching Zolah's lips, Naamah understood exactly why the girl was so frightened. "He's not here, my child," she said as she placed her arm around Zolah's trembling shoulders. "He's gone. He can't hurt you anymore. You're safe. I'm with you, daughter. I won't let him hurt you anymore. Trust me, Zolah. You must trust me."

Knowing that Zolah was in some way reliving the past, Naamah cupped her hand under the younger woman's chin and turned her face so she could look straight into her eyes. "**Let the past go, Zolah!**" she said, her voice suddenly strong and commanding. "No, don't turn your eyes away. Look at me! You must let it go. Do you understand?"

Zolah blinked once, twice. A flush of color began to creep into her cheeks. "How?" she asked. "I've tried, Mother Naamah, but I — I don't know how."

Naamah turned to look back down the ramp. Her husband and sons were almost to them now. She could waste no more time, yet she knew that some crucial divide in Zolah's life was about to be crossed. Reaching down for the small pack she carried, she pulled open its drawstrings and felt about for the one object that she now hoped would carry both her and her daughter-in-law over the threshold and into the safety of the ark.

Finding the silken cloth, she pulled it out and held it directly in front of Zolah's face. "This is how you release the past," she said as she lifted the fabric high into the air. She twirled it over her head then let it fly. The rising wind grasped at the filmy bit of fabric, then took it aloft in a flash of brilliant colors. It hung momentarily over the heads of the now entranced on-lookers, and then, as though it had suddenly taken on a life of its own, it slowly snaked its way down toward the earth. The cloth was immediately grasped by dozens of hands, each pulling in a different direction. Within seconds, there was nothing left of its gossamer threads but a few torn and filthy strands. The beauty of the cloth that Naamah had once so deeply yearned for was gone forever.

The startled look on Zolah's face told Naamah that she had indeed made her point. Without another word or a backward glance, the young woman took Naamah's hand. With heads held high, the two of them walked sedately across the threshold of the great doorway with Noah and his three sons following close behind.

With this, the crowd at the base of the ramp began to shift backward. Several of the more curious onlookers pointed toward the open doorway as though they might still see Noah and his family standing there. Others began to whisper amongst themselves. A look of fear crept into their eyes, for what they now saw in the open doorway of the ark was both terribly frightening and entirely beyond their comprehension. That great opening was aglow with a strange light! At first, the light was dim, but gradually it began to grow brighter and pulsate with an intensity that was almost blinding.

Now it was the mob's turn to panic. Those who had so recently been scoffing and threatening Noah and his family turned on their heels and ran as fast as they could away from the ark. Whatever might be happening in there, they wanted no part of it. And thus their doom was forever sealed.

Chapter Five

The Windows of Heaven Shall Open

*It was the six-hundredth year of Noah's life,
in the second month, on the seventeenth day of the month that
it happened: all of the underground springs erupted and all the
windows of heaven were thrown open. Rain poured for forty days
and forty nights. Genesis 7:11-12*

Naamah was not certain what might come next, for the door of the ark still stood agape, giving free access to anyone who might wish to charge up the ramp. She did not doubt that the vicious anger displayed by those who had once been her neighbors could easily escalate into even greater violence. She was acutely aware of the radiating light that surrounded the open doorway, but she still could not help herself from worrying about the safety of her family.

Waiting in breathless silence, Noah's three sons were equally apprehensive. Legs spread wide in a fighting stance with Japheth's cudgel at the ready, the three men positioned themselves close to the entranceway. They signaled to each other with their eyes, each one letting the other two know that no matter what might come, they would fight to the death to defend their loved ones. Minutes passed, but nothing happened. No one attempted to ascend the ramp. Not a single belligerent bystander appeared at the doorway. God's angelic host was on guard and needed no help from mere mortals to keep back the rabble.

The Women of the Ark

Finally, Japheth stepped into the opening. Shielding his eyes from the brilliant beams that radiated from the pulsing arc of light, he carefully scanned the landscape. "Ha!" he shouted with a snort of laughter, "A brave bunch this lot is! Why, look you, brothers, they've all taken off like so many frightened rabbits."

Ham stepped forward and positioned himself next to Japheth. He was as angry as he'd ever been. He, like his brother, shielded his eyes from the blinding light, but seemed not to realize that it was a heavenly host protecting them. All he could think of was how the angry mob threatened his family! He cupped his hands around his mouth and shouted out at the disappearing backs of their tormentors. "WHAT A PACK OF SCURVY CREATURES YOU ARE! YOU SCREAM YOUR INSULTS AND THREATS, BUT THERE'S NOT A MAN AMONG YOU WHO WOULD DARE STAND UP TO US!" His voice was filled with loathing, but there was a smug smile on his face.

Shem joined his brothers in the doorway. "Hush, brother," he said as he watched the last of the hecklers disappear among the trees. "It is the Lord who shall have the last word, not you," he said quietly. "Alas, I fear that they will return, for if they haven't learned of the power of Him who is with us by now, they'll never learn it. Mark my word, they'll be back!"

"There is a more vital question, my sons," said Noah as he approached Japheth and took the heavy cudgel from his hands. "How much more evidence do **you** need than that which you have seen this day? Have you not yet learned of the power of Him who is with us? What good do you think this mere stick will do against an angry mob? You have no need for such a useless weapon." He turned to face all three of his sons. "I tell you, my sons, what you need is greater faith. Faith is strong enough to beat back whatever slings and arrows the Evil One sends against us. Now go back, comfort your wives, and be at peace."

Shamed by their father's words, Ham and Japheth hung their heads and began to back away. Only Shem remained, his eyes locked onto his father's strong face. "You are God's true and faithful warrior," he said in an awed voice. "Since the days of my earliest recollections, I have seen you toil with your bare hands to build this ark. I watched you stand like an oak and take the worst that the hecklers could throw at you. I saw your head bent in prayer more times than I can ever recount. I watched your great display of patience and your burning desire to save those who refused to be saved."

Shem placed his arm around Noah's bent shoulders. "Your ways with this family are always gentle, even when we fail you," he said with deep emotion "I want you to know how proud I am to call you Father."

Then, spinning about, Shem turned and walked back into the dark shadows of the ark. He had noticed the tears that began to glisten in his father's eyes as he had been speaking, and knew with certainty that they too were a sign of Noah's great strength of character. "Dear Lord," he whispered quietly to the shadowed ceiling of the ark. "If you would but grant me a small portion of his strength, I would be content."

Noah shook his head then turned to see that Naamah had come up beside him. He gave her an encouraging smile. "Don't despair of your sons' occasional lack of faith, my dear," he said. "They're a bit rash at times, but they have staunch hearts. Faith does not always come easily to the young and headstrong, but we've taught them well. Give them time, my love. Give them time."

Trying to summon up her courage, Naamah gave Noah a weak smile. She could still feel the quivering weakness in her knees and the heavy pounding of her heart. Zolah's moments of panic had taken their toll on all of them. Glancing toward her three daughters-in-law who stood huddled together, their eyes dark with terror and their faces ashen, Naamah forced herself to take several deep breaths. These poor women had just come through an ordeal that neither she nor Noah had ever expected. What could she do to comfort them, she wondered? What could she say that would take away their moments of terror and give them the same sort of faith that she and Noah wanted for their sons?

Naamah watched her husband walk away as he followed Shem, Ham and Japheth into the ark's interior. She noticed that the shafts of sunlight that fell through the open doorway were quickly swallowed up by the many dark shadows that stalked the corridors of the cavernous vessel. A noisy clamor made by the hundreds of creatures housed within reverberated off the walls and ceiling. The animals were restless and hungry. Worse still, they were frightened, for they had heard the angry cries of the mob that had tried to storm the ramp. Their growing fear was palpable. It licked at the corners of every cage and stall. No wonder Noah and his sons had not lingered near the entrance. They had work to do, and if she were to be of any value to her family, she must rally her sons' wives from their stupor of fear and get them busy.

Looking at the three young women, Naamah realized that the challenge would not be an easy one. The beginning of their great voyage was not at all what she had envisioned. She'd been so certain that her family was well prepared. They had walked away from their home with no real regrets. They had done all that was necessary to provision the ark and prepare comfortable quarters for themselves and the animals. The amazing entry of the hundreds of creatures that were to eventually replenish the earth had been a spine-tingling experience.

But now, here they were, already in a state of disarray, and the promised flood had not even begun yet! What would become of them when the very elements began to turn violent? How would they close that massive door? How long would they be confined in this vessel before the flood would start? Where would all of the water come from? How would they manage to get along when they were cooped up with each other for months on end? The questions careened through Naamah's mind and beat against her skull, leaving her feeling dizzy and disoriented. Vaguely, she began to realize that there was an unrelenting pressure against the fingers of her right hand.

Naamah glanced down and was surprised to see Zolah clinging tightly to her hand. She tried to free herself, but the more she pulled, the tighter Zolah's grip became. Obviously, the fear was still with the poor girl.

"Zolah!" she whispered, but got no response. "ZOLAH!" Naamah shouted, for the young woman's eyes held a glassy stare. Reacting out of pain and pure reflex, Naamah thrust out her free hand and firmly shook Zolah by the shoulders. The younger woman's eyes opened wide as her head jerked back and forth.

The dazed look in Zolah's eyes cleared as she concentrated on her mother-in-law's worried face. Shaking her head as though to bring herself fully awake, she looked down at the hand that she held tightly clenched in her own, then with a sigh, she let go. "Wha— what happened?" she asked. "Where are we?" She could feel the fear creeping back, threatening to engulf her mind once more in its choking grip. She knew that Naamah would not abandon her, but she could not be certain that she had the strength to fight off the next wave of panic that was ready to pounce upon her.

"I'm sorry if I frightened you," said Naamah, "but there was no other way." She enfolded Zolah's trembling body into a tight hug. "It's all right. We're in the ark. All will be well now, child."

Zolah stood there, hesitantly, blinking at the dark shadows that seemed to grow in intensity with each passing moment. She knew that she needed to fight off the heart-gripping fear, but the darkness was pervasive. Breathing a prayer that was really a cry for help, Zolah presses her hands together in front of her face and squeezed her eyes so tightly closed that the unshed tears that swam in them were forced out onto her eyelids. "Please, Lord," she cried, "Help me. Pull me out of this blackness. Give me strength."

At that very moment, Zolah felt the soft touch of feathers brush past her face and heard a small thud just to right of her head. Turning to look in the direction of the sound, her eyes slowly adjusted to the darkness. Then, searching the floor at the base of a nearby partition, she spied the body of a small bird. The tiny creature lay crumpled and appeared lifeless. With a cry of dismay, Zolah crouched down to touch the little body. It was still warm. She bent over and pressed her trembling lips against the feathery chest as her prayer took a new turn. No longer did she plead for herself. Now she prayed that the delicate creature laying on the floor beside her might somehow survive. She prayed that, one day, when this voyage was over, it would spread its wings and fly off into the bright, blue skies of a sun-filled morning.

It was then that Rhema stepped forward. "Wait!" she said, her voice quiet but insistent. "Don't lift it up just yet, Zolah. Let me examine the poor thing first."

Zolah immediately deferred to her sister-in-law, for she knew that Rhema, like her husband Japheth, had a way with animals. Rhema knelt down and placed the tip of her index finger on the tiny bird's chest. "He's still alive," she said, "But he may be badly injured." Being ever so careful, she gently moved the bird's head. "Its neck doesn't seem to be broken," she said. Continuing her careful examination, Rhema lifted first one small wing and then the other. Finally, she gently flexed each of its spindly, little legs. "I think it's just stunned," she said as she smiled up at Zolah.

Zolah heaved a great sigh of relief. Forgetting her own paralyzing fear, she looked pleadingly at Rhema. "May I hold it?" she asked.

"Yes," answered Rhema, "But be very careful. Here, let me show you." She placed the small creature in Zolah's cupped hands. "Stroke its head gently here—that's it, just behind its eye. Be careful not to press too hard; just use the pad of your index finger."

Zolah felt an arm slip around her shoulder. Turning, she looked up into the worried face of Ophea.

"Oh, dear, it's such a fragile little thing! Are you sure it's going to be all right?" Ophea asked.

"Yes, I think so," answered Rhema. "The poor creature just needs time to rest and recover."

The three women sat there on their haunches watching the tiny bird as its eyes slowly opened. It blinked first one eye, and then the other. A trembling motion worked its way to the tips of its wings. Zolah kept her hands gently cupped around the little bird as she waited for it to fully revive.

Rhema's voice was quiet when she spoke. "Zolah, I'm so sorry for the way I acted back there on the ramp. It was a horrid thing to do! Can you ever forgive me?"

Before Zolah could answer, Ophea reached out her hand and placed it on Zolah's cheek. "Me too," she said. "I need your forgiveness too, for I was terribly cruel back there."

Zolah could feel tears stinging her eyes. "Of course, I forgive both of you," she said. "How could I not? It was because of my own stupidity that our time on that ramp was so prolonged. If I had walked quickly through the door, perhaps the crowd would have left us alone."

Zolah felt a fluttering movement in her cupped hands. Looking down, she saw that the tiny bird was now fully alert and trying desperately to free itself. "Should I let it go," she asked?

"I don't know," answered Rhema. "Perhaps there isn't enough light in here for it to see where it's going."

It was then that Zolah tilted her head back to look up at the ceiling of the ark. A sound of delight escaped her lips and then a shout of joy. "Look!" she cried. "Look up at the ceiling!"

The bright, morning sunlight was streaming through the long, narrow window that encircled the ark, below the eaves. The window was designed to provide both light and fresh air, while still keeping out the worst of the rain which was soon to fall. The luminous rays struck the underside of the roof, turning the wooden beams into a blaze of glory. Tiny sparkles of light danced and flickered across the ceiling, for droplets of resin seeping from the roof planks had dried and now hung in teardrop-shaped globes. Like miniature stars, they blanketed the underside of the ceiling, capturing within them tiny bits of sparkling sunlight.

Mesmerized by the play of sunshine and glistening resin, the three women stood there with their mouths hanging open as their eyes took in the beauty of the spectacle. It was only when the tiny bird broke free of Zolah's grasp and took off towards the shimmering ceiling that they reacted. They jumped to their feet and lifted their hands in unison toward the light. Then, letting out cries of delight, they flung their arms around each other and began to dance about in a joyous circle.

Standing to one side, Naamah smiled with pleasure as she watched her daughters-in-law celebrate. How good the Lord was! Surely, the God of Heaven had given them this special sign. Feeling a bit ashamed of the doubts and questions that had occupied her own mind just minutes earlier, she whispered a prayer asking the Lord for forgiveness. How she wished that she could be as strong in faith as her husband. But then again, perhaps that was another thing that God was giving to her—the evidence of His love so her faith would grow ever stronger.

The remainder of that first day in the ark passed uneventfully enough. Shem was right, of course. A few of the braver souls wandered back into the trampled remains of the meadow. They stared in wonder at the bright arc of light that still shimmered around the open entranceway. Speaking quietly amongst themselves, they marveled at the powerful magic that this man Noah seemed to possess. How had he managed to create a light of such radiance, they wondered, and how did he keep it going for such a long period of time? A few of the more foolhardy young men tried to step onto the ramp, but they were quickly pushed back by the brilliant beams that radiated outward from the massive doorposts.

The second day came. Still it did not rain. The skies remained clear and the breezes that cooled the land were as gentle as ever. Flocks of birds swooped over the treetops, cattle grazed peacefully on the distant hillsides. And gradually, the on-lookers returned. Before long, they managed to convince themselves that the light guarding the doorway of the ark was just one more of Noah's powerful tricks. They thought of his dire warnings of a great flood which would destroy all life on the earth, and their mocking laughter began anew.

"Say, Noah," they shouted, "Things are still nice and dry out here. Where's all of this water that you've been warning us about? We're looking up into the sky, old man, and we don't see a single drop of water falling."

The taunting went on for hours, but the family was too busy to pay any attention to it. Noah and his sons quickly realized that they would have to develop a well-coordinated system for the daily feeding and care of the animals. There were many last minute chores that needed finishing. The vines, small trees and other vegetation growing in the larger pots must to be watered, for much of this fresh growth would be necessary for their own health, as well as the feeding of many of the wild creatures housed in the ark. The potted garden had to be secured in areas where each plant might receive an optimum amount of light and air.

Having already hauled most of their own provisions into the ark's living quarters, a few final checks were needed. Naamah and her daughters-in-law had done marvels with the ark's living space, creating safety and comfort, as well as an orderliness that was pleasing to the eye. They'd made certain that the long table where their meals would be prepared and eaten had been securely fastened

The Women of the Ark

to the floorboards. Naamah was especially pleased with the various devices the men created to prevent everything from shifting about. Through much industrious effort, a large quantity of terra cotta vessels of all descriptions was accumulated. Now, the women were busily packing these vessels into boxes filled with straw, for they had gone through too much effort to have any of their fine handiwork broken during the rough stages of the voyage.

As the second day came to a close, Noah and his family noticed a distinct change in the sky. The setting sun was turning a deep shade of red—almost the color of blood. This phenomena proved even more unsettling to those outside of the ark, but their priests and leaders had returned and were now soothing their fears. "The gods are angry," they said with certainty. "But it is not because of anything we have done. They are angry over the confinement of all those innocent beasts. They find this great monstrosity that has required the cutting down of so many trees is an affront to them. Hear us, you who wish to live in peace with your gods, for nothing but complete obedience will appease their anger. They have spoken. Before the first star is seen this night, a human sacrifice must be made!"

The people shuddered at this pronouncement, but hastened to obey their priests' commands, for the western sky was now as blood red as the setting sun. Surely this was an evil omen from the angered gods! A young woman who tried to cower behind her parents was selected as the victim for the sacrificial pyre. Her hands and feet were tightly bound, and then she was lifted up onto the altar. A heavy cart bearing the large, stone idol that represented one of their fierce gods was hauled into the meadow. In their haste to carry out the ceremony, the people failed to notice the brilliant point of light that suddenly appeared in the eastern sky.

Within the ark, a new sense of urgency had descended upon the family. Something was about to happen. They could feel the change in the air, and they heard the cries of the mob as they went about their evil work just outside of the ark. Shaking with trepidation, Noah and his family gathered on the main deck and waited for the inevitable. They whispered amongst themselves, but kept an ear tuned to the outside world. Suddenly, Noah lifted his hands and called for silence. "Listen," he said. "Do you hear that?"

Everyone stood very still as they concentrated on the distant sound. Then, as though drawn by some unseen power, they moved toward the open door of the ark to see what was going on. There was a strange light in the eastern sky that seemed to be growing brighter and more concentrated by the minute. A low, rumbling sound came from the direction of that pulsing glow. The rumbling sound grew to a loud roar as the light approached, causing the very air around them to vibrate. Then, quite suddenly, the sound changed. It became a shrill, almost deafening shriek, as though some unearthly force was rushing with great speed directly toward the ark. The people outside dropped to the ground and covered their heads with their arms, while within the ark, Noah and his family retreated from the doorway, each one seeking a wooden upright or a secure post to grasp. The powerful beam of light streaked across the open meadow and slammed against the door of the ark with such force that, despite the massive logs that held the vessel in place, its entire structure shook violently. And with a final groan, the great door fell heavily into place. No human hands could have done such a thing. The time had indeed come. The door of the ark was closed and sealed by the mighty hand of God![13]

Appalled by what they had just witnessed and certain that the anger of their gods would not be appeased now unless they killed Noah and his entire family, the mob rushed toward the ark. A call went out for strong men to come and help pry open the massive door. The commotion grew ever more frantic, but try as they might, no amount of effort by their strongest men could budge the heavy door. Finally, even the religious leaders gave up in disgust.

On the seventh day, the world outside of the ark began to change. Ominous clouds started to form in the firmament above the earth. The clouds boiled over each other and massed in great profusion on the horizon as they built in height and density. Within minutes, they turned as black as a crow's wing. Then a strong wind began to blow, coming first from the east, and then the west, bending down the trees and sending their leaves scattering across the landscape. Soon they were caught up into a swirling vortex of wind and debris.

Inside the ark, Noah and his family collectively held their breaths as they sought out secure spots where they could await the coming fury. Strangely, the creatures housed within the ark all seemed to have fallen into a deep stupor. The birds were huddled on the floors of their cages, their heads under their wings, and their feet curled up into their feathers. The larger animals were hunkered down in their stalls, their eyes closed and their breathing slow and shallow. The interior of the ark became oddly silent. Naamah glanced at her husband and nodded her head. The look in his eyes told her that God, in His mercy, had surely seen to it that the creatures within the ark would not be harmed by the violence that was about to take place.

Outside, the winds grew steadily in strength and velocity. The people gathered in the meadow ceased their bloodthirsty sacrifices as stunned looks of fear began to creep across their faces. A succession of deep, rumbling sounds was heard in the distance. Was there another great herd of animals coming toward them? They lifted their hands above their eyes and scanned the distant horizon. No, they could see no tell-tale dust clouds! There was something very different happening—something they had never experienced before.

First a moment of silence, when nothing seemed to stir. Then, in a heart-stopping display, the roiling bank of clouds suddenly erupted with such brilliant light that it seemed as though they had caught on fire. Jagged tongues of super-heated flames spewed out of them. The rumbling grew louder. Blinding flashes of lightning jumped from one great cloudbank to the other, setting each one, in turn, afire. The terrified people could feel the ground begin to tremble and shake under their feet as huge bolts of lightening shot out of the bottom of the clouds and crashed into the earth, splintering everything in their path.

Then the first drops of rain began to fall. At first the rain came lightly, but it quickly grew to great sheets of water that raced across the ground, obliterating the horizon and even the nearby tree line. The meadow was soon awash as the pelting rain filled all of the low spots. The winds moaned and screamed as though many wild beasts were entrapped in them. A massive cyclone of wind, water, and all manner of debris formed in the sky above the heads of the cowering people. It roared toward them. Skipping erratically along the earth, the growing cyclone sucked up everything in its path. It ripped out hoary, old trees as though they were nothing but splinters and tore them into shreds. It siphoned up dirt, gouging out a great path of destruction as it moved across the landscape.

Pushing and shoving aside those who stood in their way, the terrified onlookers began to race toward the ark. Their religious leaders, who had just hours earlier incited their followers against Noah and his family, were now the first to begin pounding upon the sides of the great wooden structure. Old people and young children were thrown to the ground and trampled by the terrified mob. Women screeched in terror and forgot their own children in their haste to find a place of safety. Grown men, their muscular arms used as battering rams, frantically pounded upon the door of the ark. "LET US IN, NOAH!" they screamed. "HAVE MERCY UPON US! PLEASE, OLD MAN, HAVE MERCY AND LET US IN!"

But the door did not open. The water came down from the sky in torrents, and then the earth itself began to moan and scream out as great cracks and crevices split apart the ground under the feet of the panicked multitude. Scalding water and hot gases burst forth from the deepest crevices of the earth. Great geysers of water shot up hundreds of feet into the air. Terrified animals and people ran first one way then the other as the devastating forces of nature did their horrific work of destruction. Humans and animals alike soon were swept along by the swirling waters or swallowed up as the ground under their feet tore apart. The earth and sky groaned as though in great pain, drowning out the sounds of the wailing people and screaming animals.

Within the ark, the family of Noah stood in speechless horror. They could hear many frantic hands clawing at the undersides of the vessel and the terrified cries for help. Ophea squeezed her eyes shut and pressed her hands tightly against her ears. Rhema fell to the floor with her arms clasped tightly over her head. Zolah and Naamah clung to each other, tears coursing down their cheeks. Noah and his three sons, too stunned to do anything else, held onto the wooden posts that stood on either side of the doorway. Never in their wildest imaginations had they envisioned that the time of destruction would begin with such terrifying force!

Gradually, the ark began to shudder and then shift from one side to the other as the rising waters lifted it off its supporting beams. The screams of the people outside of the great vessel began to lessen, and then fade away. The floorboards creaked as the waters rose, but the ark held steady. Soon, the sounds of rushing water obliterated even the screeching of the wind. But within the ark, all was dry and secure. [14]

Noah reached down and gently pulled Naamah to her feet. "Wife," he said, his voice filled with both tenderness and sorrow, "It has begun." There were tears in his eyes, for though he had done everything he could to warn the people of God's judgment, he still felt great sorrow for their loss.

Naamah could only sob as she laid her head upon Noah's heaving chest and wrapped her arms about his waist. She heard the steady thudding of his heart. Somehow, this reassuring sound began to calm her. "I never envisioned that it would be this bad," she said in a choked whisper.

Resting his chin on the top of his wife's head, Noah unashamedly let his tears drop into her graying hair. "I know," he said as he gently stroked her back. "I know."

They stood there, wrapped in each other's arms, as the waters rose higher and the great waves of the flood washed every living thing outside of the ark into the awful maelstrom.

Chapter Six

And the Waters Shall Cover the Earth

The flood continued forty days and the waters rose and lifted the ship high over the Earth. The waters kept rising, the flood deepened on the Earth, the ship floated on the surface. The flood got worse until all the highest mountains were covered—the high water mark reached twenty feet above the crest of the mountains. Everything died. Anything that moved—dead. Birds, farm animals, wild animals, the entire teeming exuberance of life—dead. And all people—dead. Every living, breathing creature that lived on dry land died, he wiped out the whole works—people and animals, crawling creatures and flying birds, every last one of them, gone. Only Noah and his company on the ship lived. The floodwaters took over for 150 days. Genesis 7:17-23

Violent winds continued to whip and churn the rising water into monstrous waves that battered the ark for day after long day. Torrential rains pounded its roof and swept along its wooden sides in wind-driven sheets. The eerie sounds made by wind and water echoed from one end of the great vessel to the other as it moved aimlessly upon the surface of the deluge. Each plank and beam on the ark creaked and groaned, and as the great vessel swung one way and then the other, a deep shudder traveled the entire length of its long hull.

The Women of the Ark

The people and animals aboard the ark cowered in fear as the cataclysm raged on. Noah was especially tense, his faith tried as it had never been tried before. If the vessel should begin to succumb to the violent winds and pounding waves, surely they would all be lost, but he and his family could do little more than hold on for dear life and pray that the worst would soon be over. Sleep was impossible. Screeching winds reverberated throughout the vast interior of the ark. Flashes of lightening and ear-splitting crashes of thunder traveled from horizon to watery horizon, pounding at the vessel as though it were a taut drum.

The family could not manage to eat but a few morsels of food, for if they were to unfasten even a small cask or pottery jar, a sudden violent shift in the movement of the ark might send the container hurtling through the great ship like a lethal weapon. From time to time, they managed to swallow a few sips of liquid from the water-proof pouches that hung about their waists.

Feeding the animals was an almost impossible chore. Fortunately, before the worst of the violent weather began, they'd managed to fill most of the feeding trays and bins. It was doubtful, of course, that the poor creatures were any more in a state to digest food than were the people.

During those first few days, Japheth was greatly concerned about how they would quench the thirst of the many creatures aboard the ark, for the system that Shem had devised to lighten this task was not altogether effective under such violent conditions. Prior to their entry into the ark, Shem had created an ingenious aqueduct system for supplying water to the various pens and cages. By cutting large bamboo poles in half lengthwise, joining them tightly together, then hanging them from long strips of rawhide that were secured to the rafters beneath each deck, they were able to provide drinking water to the hundreds of pens and cages without spending hours lugging heavy buckets about. But now, with the storm raging day after day, the aqueduct system was only partially effective. With each violent thrust of wind or waves, the fresh water sloshed over the sides of the bamboo tubes, accumulating in large puddles on the floorboards. Wide rivulets of water ran across the planks and dripped over the edges of the decks. The seeping water picked up loose bits of straw and hay as it ran along the decks, creating a quagmire wherever it gathered. The combination of wet wood and sodden particles of fodder made the walkways so slippery that men and animals alike had all they could do to remain upright.

Despite these problems, as the hours and days passed and the storm raged on, Noah and his sons began to truly appreciate how perfect the structural integrity of the great ship was. No matter how violent the gales or powerful the waves, the ark held firm. Nothing but divine wisdom could have devised such an amazing vessel! And though their physical discomforts were difficult to bear, nothing could compare to the terrible losses of life that had gone on outside of this safe haven that God had planned for them.

As the floodwaters rose ever higher, the family occasionally heard odd, scraping noises on the underside of the vessel. Was it possible that someone was still alive out there? No, surely not! Nothing could have survived those first few days of the wild maelstrom! Listening intently to the strange sounds, they began to realize that what they were hearing must be trees that had been uprooted and were now being swept along by the rushing waters. Climbing to the uppermost deck, they pried up a small corner section of the stiff leather that covered the narrow airspace running just below the roof hoping for a glimpse of what sort of objects were floating by, but blinding sheets of rain obliterated their view.

Though there was no means of steering this great ship, the flat-bottomed ark rode the great swells of foaming water with a steadiness that was truly amazing. Occasionally its inhabitants could feel the ark swing about as the directions of the winds changed or the swells of the flood washed along mountain peaks that had not yet been swallowed up by the rising water. The massive, seasoned logs that had been used to form the ark's hull acted as ballast to keep the vessel riding low in the water. After those first few days of concern, Noah and his sons felt comforted that their ship was not about to capsize, nor would it be swamped by the great swells of turbulent water that washed over it.

But from the beginning, the sounds coming from the outside of the ark had caused them the greatest heartache. Those terror-filled screams of drowning people and animals still rang in their ears. The clawing of desperate hands on the outer planking, the screeching of the wind, the explosive sounds of the earth being shattered and torn would forever haunt them. Whatever might befall them in the years to come, the horrific beginnings of the world-shattering flood would be vividly replayed again and again in their memories.

While Noah and his sons tried to cover their fears with hard work, their womenfolk were the ones who suffered the most. Naamah tried her best to remain courageous and strong, but the surging waves of nausea that had engulfed her as the ark began to float free, days later, still held her in their terrible grip. She lay prostrate upon her sleeping pallet with a damp cloth pressed against her forehead, for the continuing nausea and series of pounding headaches sapped the last bit of her strength.

Ever solicitous of his wife's troubles, Noah sat beside Naamah and tried to coax her to swallow a few sips of tepid broth. Naamah opened her eyes, but their listless appearance and the dark shadows that pooled beneath them told her husband that she was not yet ready to face her family or take up the many chores that so desperately needed to be done. Naamah shook her head at the proffered cup.

"Naamah, my love," Noah pleaded, "You must rouse yourself. You cannot simply lie here and waste away. Think of the others. Think of your sons and their wives. They need you; Naamah, I need you!"

With an obvious struggle, Naamah turned to face her husband. "Where are the others?" she asked, her voice so weak that she could speak only in a low whisper. "Where are my beloved daughters?"

Noah smiled at this title of endearment, for certainly his son's wives had become as close to Naamah as though they were her own flesh and blood. "They, too, have taken to their beds," he answered. "But you need not worry about them, for they are strong, young women with a determination to survive. Once the worst of these storms has passed, they'll be up and busy again, as you will, my dear, if only you'll take a bit of nourishment.

"I cannot bear even the thought of food," cried Naamah, "But I would love a cool drink of water."

Encouraged by this simple request, Noah hastened off to fetch a cup. Returning to his wife's bedside, he gently lifted her head and placed the cup of water against her parched lips.

Her thirst quenched, Naamah fell back against the soft, fleece pillow and closed her eyes. Noah rubbed her arm and began to hum a tune that Shem had composed several months earlier. He knew it to be one of her favorite pieces, one that would have a soothing effect. Within minutes, Naamah fell into a deep and restful sleep.

Several hours passed. When next she awoke, Naamah found someone else seated on the edge of her sleeping mat. She smiled when she saw it was none other than Zolah.

"Are you feeling better, Mother?" Zolah asked.

Naamah looked up into the drawn face of her daughter-in-law and realized that she, too, must have gone through several days of sickness. Zolah's face held a white pallor, and her cheeks seemed hollowed out so the fine bones that lay beneath were clearly visible.

Rousing herself, Naamah tried to sit upright, but her head swirled so badly that it was all she could do not to fall backward again. "I'm glad to see you, Zolah," she said. "But you look so tired."

"No more than you, Mother. This has not been an easy experience for any of us."

Naamah nodded. "What has happened to Ophea and Rhema?" she asked. "Are they sick also?"

Zolah smiled and then began to giggle mischievously. "Rhema is hunkered down in the stall with the horses," she answered. "I think she's come to the conclusion that they are the only beings on this ark fit to live with. And as for Ophea, well, all we've seen of her for days now are the bottoms of her feet. She's wedged herself into a cupboard and vows not to come out until this boat rests once more upon dry land!"

"WHAT!" exclaimed Naamah, as she struggled to come to a standing position. "Surely you are teasing me, Zolah!"

"Well—perhaps I'm stretching the truth just a wee bit," answered Zolah, the mischievous smile still pulling at the corners of her mouth, "But as you can see, you are now standing upright, and there is a definite flash of fire in your voice."

Naamah playfully patted Zolah's hands. "Why, you little vixen!" she said. "Now tell me the truth. Where are my other daughters?"

Zolah shrugged as the smile left her face. "In truth, Mother, this ordeal has laid them rather low. The terror of those first few days

The Women of the Ark

almost paralyzed them with fright. They're doing better now, but for a time there—well, it is not something that I can easily talk about."

"And you, child?" Naamah searched Zolah's face. "What of your own fears?"

Zolah looked down at the floor and shook her head from side to side. "It was horrible," she whispered. "But perhaps I'm accustomed to facing violence, Mother Naamah."

Zolah looked up then, her eyes filling with tears. "Oh, Mother Naamah, it was the most terrifying thing I have ever experienced, but—but somehow, I found that I had the strength to face it without going into a blind panic. Does that seem strange to you? Does it seem odd that I was standing there like a pillar of stone when we were entering this ark, but when the very worst of the storm was raging, I was somehow able to conquer my fears?"

Naamah smiled at the young woman who stood before her. "No," she answered. "It is not strange at all. The experience on the ramp, and then, when you reacted to that little, stunned bird—oh, Zolah, dear child, surely that must have been a moment of truth for you. I think perhaps you've learned to turn and face your fears rather than withering before them. It is God's doing, of course, but it's also because you were willing to let Him make a change in your life."

Naamah laid her hands gently on either side of Zolah's face. "I have said this before, child, but now I'm more convinced than ever. God has some great purpose for your life. It may be many years before you understand what that purpose is, but when it comes, I'm certain that you'll be ready for it."

Naamah reached out for Zolah's arm. "Here, child," she said. "Lend me a hand, won't you? My poor old legs still feel so weak."

Arm in arm, the two women left the sleeping quarters and headed to the kitchen area. "What everyone needs now," said Naamah, "is a good, hot meal. Now get yourself down that ladder, my dear, and see if you can rouse the rest of the family while I get a fire going."

First, Naamah placed some bits of kindling in the large, stone crucible that her talented husband had chiseled out for her. By using clay to securely mount the heavy bowl onto thick slabs of slate, Noah had designed a fire pit that would provide a safe and easily accessible area for both meal preparation and warmth. He had even constructed a small oven out of clay and rock, setting it securely against the outer wall next to the fire pit and building smoke shafts for both up through the open space just under the roof.

Naamah knew that she must be very cautious about building fires within the ark. If sparks should fly into the air, they could easily set fire to the vessel's wooden planks. The dried fodder for the feeding of the animals was especially dangerous, for there was hardly a crevice or corner in the ark where it wasn't stored. It caught on their clothing and lodged in their hair and beards. It tracked about on their sandals, and when one of the large bales were torn apart, its particles flew through the air in yellow clouds of choking dust.

Thus, when Japheth entered the kitchen quarters, having just finished feeding the elephants and giraffes, Naamah immediately shooed him out, insisting that he must first shake off every last bit of clinging hay before he could enter her kitchen. One by one, as each family member approached, they were greeted by the same, firm admonition. Not even Noah was exempt from his wife's tongue lashing when he failed to notice a small clump of straw that had attached itself to the hem of his robe.

"I have no intention of surviving these terrible storms only to have this ark burn down around our ears!" Naamah said in a voice that brooked no argument. "And while I'm in charge of this kitchen, the lot of you will obey my rules, or you'll find yourselves eating down there in one of the animal stalls!"

Ham let out a snort and slapped Japheth on the back. "Well now, brother," he said with a roaring laugh. "Do you hear the woman? It sounds to me like our dear mother has recovered quite nicely from her queasy stomach!"

At the end of her patience, Naamah reacted. She spun around and lifted her hand to shake a finger in Ham's face. "Now you listen to me, young man," she said, her eyes boring into his, "I'll tolerate no disrespect! You may make fun of the apes and mock the hyenas, if you wish, but I am still your mother so you'd best remember to keep a civil tongue in your head when you speak to me!" Chagrined, Ham backed toward the doorway. Though he was a muscular man who stood a good five hands taller than his mother, he knew when he had met his match.

The Women of the Ark

While the family planted themselves about the wide table that sat to one side of the large kitchen area, Naamah busied herself in the preparation of a simple but nourishing meal. She ordered the younger women to go to the storage bins and pull out some of the fresh vegetables, roots, and legumes. Before long, she had a thick stew boiling away, sending up a wonderful aroma. She added a few sprigs from several bunches of dried herbs that hung in profusion from the rafters of the storage area.

In the meantime, Ophea prepared a large platter of unleavened bread, which she baked in the small oven that sat against the outer wall of the ark. Rhema managed to milk one of the goats. Carefully balancing the pottery flask on one hip, she climbed the ladder to the kitchen quarters then triumphantly held her offering aloft as smiles broke out on the faces of the assembled company. Zolah brought in a bowl filled with dates, figs and dark, purple grapes. She placed it in the center of the table, then went back to the storage area to get a wedge of cheese, which she deftly sliced into small, bite-size pieces.

It was when they all sat down to eat this, their first real meal in the ark, that they realized that the storm had started to abate. The winds no longer tore at the roof planks, the rolling swells seemed to have subsided, and the reverberating peals of thunder now sounded distant. The rain was still falling, though now it was not blowing across the floodwaters in blinding sheets. They could hear raindrops pelting on the roof, but even that was reduced to a sound that was actually quite pleasant.

Noah tore off a large chunk of bread, rose to his feet, and lifted his arms up in prayer. "Dear Lord," he said, in deep, resonant tones that echoed across the wide room, "You have brought us this far through turmoil, flood and mighty storms. You have given us this great vessel—this ark of safety and deliverance. We praise Your holy name, Lord, and lift up our arms in supplication and prayer. Bless this feast that, in Your great mercy, You have laid before us. May it nourish our bodies and quicken our minds. Let us never forget that it is You, O' Righteous God, who is the creator and sustainer of all life. Strengthen our faith and quicken our resolve to ever remain true to the Most Holy God of all heaven and earth."

Then, opening his eyes and looking from one to the other of his loved ones, his face broke out into a broad smile. "Eat, my children," he said. "Fill your stomachs with this bounty that God has given us!"

No one needed a second invitation. They fell upon the food, and reveled in the fact that they were actually hungry. When at last they had sated themselves, they leaned onto the table and talked for hours about what they would do when they were once more upon dry land. Finally, Shem went to his sleeping quarters and brought out his lyre. Japheth pulled from his tunic a simple flute that he had fashioned out of a reed, and Ham, who above all else, loved rhythm, used a leather-covered clay pot as a drum. Spontaneously, everyone began to sing to the music that the young men played with such wonderful abandon. They sang many of the songs that they already knew, and they made up new ones as they went along. They told the old stories of the days when the earth was new—those wonderful stories of the Garden of Eden that Noah's father had heard directly from the lips of Adam. The oil lamps flickered against the walls, and the fire in the stone crucible sent out a warm glow that danced across the faces of the assembled family members. Finally, they were at peace with the world around them, even if that world was covered with water.

This was the first of many meals they were to have on the ark. Their food was simple, but nourishing. They ate no meat, for their diet supplied them with everything they needed. They clearly understood that their commission from God was to save the animals of the ark, not devour them. The knowledge of how to properly prepare and balance their meals was vital to their survival on the long voyage that lay ahead. This instruction had come down to them from Adam and Eve, those first parents, who had known the perfection of the Garden of Eden where there was no death. Thus, nuts, legumes, roots, grains, fruits, vegetables, and other nutritious foods were the staple diet on the ark. [15]

The preservation of the foodstuff needed for themselves, as well as the animals, was an all-consuming job left mostly to the women. Naamah was rightfully proud of what she and her daughters-in-law had accomplished prior to their entering the ark. Their mealtimes became their most important social events. It was a time to rest and talk over the accomplishments of the day. Their closeness as a family unit was even stronger when they sat down to break bread together. And no matter how tiring the work or dismal the long, dark days, when they gathered around the cooking fire and breathed in the fragrant aromas that filled Naamah's kitchen, peace and contentment settled over them like a warm blanket.

One morning, exactly forty days after they had entered the ark, the family awoke to the glorious sight of brilliant sunshine coming through the long, high window. Once again, the undersurface of the roof began to sparkle with light. Beams of sunlight touched the cages on the uppermost levels and filtered down through the cracks and crevices to the decks below. The air, which had become so terribly foul over the past few weeks, now held a subtle but refreshing change. Collectively, every living creature on the ark seemed to be taking a deep breath.

Tumbling out of their sleeping pallets, the family headed for the ladder that led to the upper deck. Quickly, they began rolling up the leather shades that covered one section of the long window. Pure air wafted through the ark and circulated freely as a freshening breeze moved the massive vessel along the surface of the now tranquil floodwaters.

Peering out onto a drowned world where nothing but water could be seen from horizon to horizon, the family was aghast at the seemingly endlessness of the flood. But as their eyes adjusted to the bright sunlight, they could not help but marvel at the beauty that surrounded them. Above them was an azure blue sky filled with puffy clouds that floated effortlessly across the dome of the heavens. Banks of clouds that had massed along the distant horizons were reflected in the water creating a breathtaking double image. The cloud formations that hung above them were filled with color—white and soft yellow on their tops, and their undersides were painted in soft pastels. Sunlight streamed in great golden bands through breaks in the cloud cover. And upon the surface of the water, sunlight sparkled and glistened like a firmament filled with millions of twinkling stars.

There were other sensations that reached them, making them feel that a change was surely on its way. The air had a fresh, tangy smell to it, and when they licked their lips, they tasted salt. What strange things had happened to the world they had once known? What might lay ahead of them in the days and months to come? And having come this far, having survived the cataclysmic events that had so altered the earth, they knew with renewed certainty, that no matter what might happen next, their futures lay safely in God's hands.

Chapter Seven

Alone Upon the Waters

*God, my God, how great you are! Beautifully, gloriously robed, dressed up in sunshine, and all heaven stretched out for your tent. You built your palace on the ocean deeps, made a chariot out of clouds and took off on wind-wings. You commandeered winds as messengers, appointed fire and flame as ambassadors.
You set earth on a firm foundation So that nothing can shake it, ever. You blanketed earth with ocean, covered the mountains with deep waters . . . Psalms 104:2-6*

The elderly couple stood on the upper deck with their arms about each other as they gazed out into a night sky spangled with starlight. A quarter moon hung low in the western sky, but its illumination was not bright enough to wash out the brilliant points of light that filled the black canopy of the heavens. Every so often, a shooting star would blaze across the sky, trailing behind it a fiery tail.

Suddenly, Naamah turned her hand palm upward and stretched her arm as far out of the window as she could, then letting out a soft laugh. "Oh, I thought for certain I might catch that one!" she exclaimed. Turning to face her husband, Naamah gave him a shy smile.

"You are an incredible woman!" Noah said as he chuckled and pulled her tightly to his side. He pressed his chin against the top of her head and breathed in the fragrance of her hair. Newly washed, if he was not mistaken, and it faintly smelled of a mixture of aloe and dried clover. Naamah was forever experimenting with her various potted plants and herbs. In most cases, her concoctions were harmless, although they caused at least one close call when she'd mixed up a batch of dried herbs that she was certain would cure the flux, only to find out that it did just the opposite. Noah smiled to himself at the memory of that small disaster.

"You can't catch a star, my love," he said, "Not even a falling one. And even if you could, what would you do with it once you had it?"

"Oh, I don't know," answered Naamah. "Perhaps I'd hang it from one of the rafters so we could watch it twinkle and shine right here inside the ark. Wouldn't that be lovely?"

"But, Naamah, aren't you the one who is so afraid of sparks?" said Noah. "If a single spark could start a fire that would burn this ark down around our ears, as you've often warned us, can you just imagine what a star would do?"

"Hmm," answered Naamah. "That's something I'll have to think about. But, just look, Husband. Look at how bright the stars are. It almost seems that they are close enough to touch."

"Yes," answered Noah. "They are lovely. God has created such beauty for us to enjoy, even now with the floodwaters covering the earth. What a glorious time it will be when we can stand on dry land and watch the stars twinkling above us!" He rubbed his face into her hair. "I long for that day, just as you do."

Taking Naamah's hands in his, Noah suddenly realized that her fingers were trembling. Turning to look at her more closely, he saw that his wife's enjoyment of the night sky had vanished. "Are you all right, my love?" he asked. "Why, look at you; your teeth are chattering. What's wrong?"

"I'm just a bit chilly, that's all," she answered as she pulled away from him. "Husband," she asked. "How much longer do you think it will be? We've been on this vessel for months now." Turning away, she briskly rubbed her upper arms, then turned back to face her husband. "I—I don't want to be impatient, Noah. And I am thankful that the worst of the storms are over, but—but how much longer must we live like this? How long will it take for the waters to subside?"

Noah let out a deep sigh and shook his head. "I'm afraid that it may still be a very long time before that happens, my dear." He walked toward her and held out his hands. "Come," he said. "Let me warm you." Once again he wrapped his arms around her and could feel her entire body shivering. "Naamah, my love, I know how hard this has been for you," he said. "But we must try to be patient just a little longer." He lifted her chin and looked lovingly into her eyes. "You're a good woman, Naamah. You're everything that I could have ever asked for in a wife. The end of this journey **will** come, I promise you that, but it must be in God's time, not ours. You understand that, don't you, my love?"

Naamah nodded and gave him a weak smile. "Yes, Husband, I understand, but it's hard—so very hard to be patient."

"I know," answered Noah. "But it is not our place to question God's will. He knows what's best. Some day soon, my dear wife, we shall all stand together on dry land and look back on this experience with wonder and thankfulness. But for now, we must simply trust that He is doing what is best for us."

Naamah dropped her eyes and nodded again. "I know that," she said, and I promise that I will try my best." Lifting her chin, she looked at Noah with such trust that it both thrilled and frightened him. "Oh, my dear husband, what would we do without your faith?" she asked. Rising up on tiptoe, she planted a gentle kiss on his bearded cheek, then pulled away and wrapped her arms around herself. "Brrr," she said as a shiver ran through her. "It's getting so cold! The nights are changing, Noah. I don't ever remember them being so cold before."

Noah reached out to pull Naamah's shawl closely about her neck, then pulled off his own cloak and wrapped it around her shoulders. "Come," he said. "Let's get you out of this damp air. We'll go down to the kitchen and build up a nice, hot fire. You'll feel better once you're warmed up."

When they reached the top of the ladder that led to their living quarters, Noah turned to help Naamah climb down the wide rungs. Once at the bottom, he stopped and rubbed her hands briskly between his. "You know, my love, you're right, the nights have gotten much colder. I'm not certain, but I think all of the rain must have had something to do with it."

Noah, of course, did not understand the full extent of the vast changes that the cataclysm had brought upon the earth. The protective vapor canopy that had, before the flood, covered the planet like a warm blanket, holding in the heat of the sun and maintaining a constant, temperate climate, had literally collapsed. And there had also been vast alterations to the layers of the earth itself, for its surface had been torn apart by horrendous volcanic eruptions and the shifting of massive geological plates. In time, Noah and his family would experience weather changes that mankind had never known before.

As the family members huddled close to the fire, wrapping themselves in fleeces and holding their outstretched hands to the glowing flames, they could find little to be cheerful about. No one seemed interested in conversation, let alone their usual evening occupation of storytelling. Shem, Ham and Japheth had climbed to the upper deck to make sure that the leather shades were tightly secured, but drafts of frosty air still seeped into the ark, leaving them all feeling cold and out of sorts.

As was his custom, Noah led them in prayer and worship before they headed off to their various sleeping quarters. But as they walked single file along the narrow passageway, Noah stopped and held up his hand. "Listen," he said, "Do you hear that?"

No one needed to answer, for the intensity of the wind had increased, and from the sound of it, it was now laced with something more than just rain. Throwing off his fleece cloak, Japheth picked up a small oil lamp and climbed the ladder to the upper deck. He untied one of the leather shades, pulled up a corner, and thrust his arm out into the night air. Just as quickly, he jerked it back. What was that cold, prickling sensation, he wondered? Had he been stung by a swarm of hornets? No, of course not. If it were hornets, he would have immediately felt heat from the poison of their stings.

Curious now, he stuck his arm outside once again, then pulled it back to examine what lay on his bare skin. "Ho, there!" he exclaimed as he looked at the tiny, white crystals covering his forearm. "What's this?" Lightly touching one of the delicate flakes with the tip of his finger, he was amazed to find that it simply disappeared. He held the lamp close to his arm. One by one, as the warmth from the oil lamp touched the strange crystals, they appeared to melt and turn into tiny droplets of water.

Excited by his discovery, Japheth shouted out for the others. "Father, Shem, Ham, come up here. There is something happening outside that you must see!"

The three men climbed the ladder and looked at Japheth with questioning eyes. "Stick your arms out the window," he said. "Go ahead, pull up your sleeves and stick your arms out of the window."

Each man did as Japheth had ordered, and just as quickly jerked his arm back again. "What is this strange powder?" asked Ham examining his arm in the flickering light of the lamp. "Ah, it's so cold on my skin!"

"Look more closely," said Japheth as he lifted the lantern so they could examine their arms. "It's not a powder," he said. "It's crystals, some sort of very cold but beautiful crystals."

Shem was turning his arm first one way, then the other. "They really are beautiful," he said as he examined the melting flakes. "Look at all of the different shapes and patterns. But they don't last very long. What a shame; I'd like to save some of them to show Zolah."

"Whatever it is," said Noah, with a smile on his face, "we shall have to think of a name for it."

Snow, ice, and sleet had never been known to fall on the earth before the flood. Noah and his sons were experiencing their very first taste of winter. And because they were riding the top of the floodwaters, which now covered the tallest mountains, they were floating along at an extremely high elevation.

Despite the biting cold, Shem knew that Zolah would want to see this new discovery. He turned to call for her to climb the ladder, but before he could get the words out of his mouth, she was at his side. And coming up behind her were the other women.

"What are you up to?" Zolah asked. "We could hear the excitement in your voices and decided that we just had to see what was going on up here."

Without saying a word, Shem pulled up the sleeve of Zolah's robe, grasped her bare arm and pushed it out into the cold night air.

"**OW!** Shem, what are you doing? It's cold out there!" She yanked her arm back in then looked down at it in wonder. "What is this?" she asked. "I've never seen anything like this before!"

"Right," answered Shem as he began to roll up one of the leather shades. As the family stood there looking out into the night, shafts of pearly-white moonlight began to peek through the scudding clouds. The stars were gone now, covered by the fast-moving clouds, but the air was filled with millions of the fast-moving, white flurries. The soft moonlight touched the delicate snow flakes causing them to glitter with such rare beauty, that despite the intense cold, the family stood there mesmerized by the sight.

They went to bed that night dreaming of what they had seen. The next morning they found the outside air so frigid that that they no longer had any desire to experiment with the white flakes that now lay in small wind-blown mounds on the lower ledges of the window. Worried about the birds and smaller animals, Naamah insisted that their cages must be moved to warmer locations in the ark. It took most of the morning to complete the task, leaving them little time for anything else other than feeding the rest of the animals.

The next day was just as cold, and the day after that. The novelty of their first snowstorm quickly wore off, for now the black clouds were as likely to drop a freezing rain as the lovely snowflakes.

Then, one bitterly cold evening just after they'd finished eating their supper, an especially heavy gust of frigid wind slammed into the ark with such force that the entire vessel shuddered from stem to stern. Exasperated by the long days and nights of confinement, and now the added discomfort of the biting cold, Ham slammed his hands down onto the table as he pushed himself upright. "WILL THIS NEVER END?" he shouted.

Grabbing his wife's arm, Ham pulled her roughly toward their sleeping quarters. Before pulling down the leather flap that covered the doorway, he spun around and faced his father with a look on his face that Noah had never seen before. "You and your constant talk of patience and faith!" He spit the words out through clenched teeth. "How much more of this must we go through, Father, before your God is satisfied? How much longer does He intend to punish us?"

Without waiting for an answer, Ham jerked down the flap and tied it securely from the inside.

Noah could only stand there with his mouth open and a look of pain on his face. "Ham, my son," he started to say, but Naamah reached for his arm and pulled him away.

"No," she said as she shook her head with sadness. "Leave it for now, Husband, for you will only make him angrier. Speak to him in the morning when he has had time to calm down."

Noah's troubled expression wrenched at her heart, but she knew Ham too well to think that any further appeal on the part of his father would be useful.

"What is happening to him?" asked Noah as they made their way to their own quarters. "How can he say such things when it is God who has saved us from destruction?"

"He's not himself right now," said Naamah. "It was his anger and frustration that was talking. He'll be all right in the morning." Naamah gazed into her husband's eyes, and with a saddened heart, she realized that he was looking very old and frail of late. Reaching out to grasp his trembling hands, she squeezed them gently, than reached up and touched his face. "You'll see, he'll be all right in the morning, my love," she said, her voice low so the others would not hear. "I'm certain that he'll be sorry for his outburst and ask for your forgiveness." Naamah smiled at Noah, hoping that her words would prove true, but in her heart she felt a cold chill. She knew that underneath her brave front, there was a nagging fear that Ham had meant every angry word that he had uttered.

"Yes, perhaps you're right," said Noah, though there were tears in his eyes. "I'll talk to him in the morning." He patted Naamah's hand. "You know, I think he's just overtired. I was watching him and Shem this morning. They were trying to hoist one of those big bales of hay up from the lower storage area and having a hard time of it. It was obviously much too heavy for them." Noah began to smile. "You know what happened, my love?" he asked.

Naamah shook her head. "No, husband, what happened?"

"Well, no matter how hard they tried, they couldn't get that bale of hay out of the hold. Then along came Japheth riding on the back of that big, bull elephant. Before they knew what was happening, that great beast had shoved the two of them aside with a swipe of his trunk."

Naamah began to laugh. "Husband, do you remember when that old bull threw the poor fellow off the ramp? I can still see the look on his face when he landed on the ground and found himself staring into the eyes of that angry elephant!"

"Yes," said Noah, his mood apparently lightened by the memory. "Well, let me tell you, that same elephant is worth his weight in gold. After putting Ham and Shem in their places, he wrapped his trunk around that bale of hay and lifted it out like it was a small pile of twigs!" Noah laughed as he recalled the site of Japheth sitting atop the elephant, prodding it along as Ham and Shem lay there with the wind knocked out of them.

When they reached their sleeping compartment, Noah slid his arm around Naamah and pushed the loose strands of hair back from her face. His smile slowly faded and his eyes grew troubled once more. "I have been praying for Ham," he said. "He's a bit like the weather, you know, very changeable." Noah shook his head sadly. "It's strange, my dear, but of late my youngest son seems to go out of his way to defy me."

Naamah closed her eyes and rubbed her forehead with her hand. Oh, yes, she too had seen the changes in Ham. He had always been impatient, reacting rashly to things that did not please him rather than stopping to think how his bitter words and impulsive behavior might bring pain to those who loved him. The jealousy he had sometimes exhibited towards his two older brothers had often been the cause of friction, giving Naamah much worry, but never before had she seen him act quite so irreverently toward his father. The persistent thought that Ham's rebellious behavior would one day cause both her and Noah a great heartache would not leave her. She loved Ham as dearly as she loved her other two sons, but now, like Noah, Ham's growing surliness caused her great concern. She prayed that, once they were back on dry land, he would again be a loving son to them and a gentle, caring husband to Ophea.

Poor Ophea! Her quiet demeanor was no match for Ham's increasingly angry outbursts. As the days passed, both Noah and Naamah became alarmed at Ham's behavior toward his wife. It was obvious that he did not respect her, for he would often speak to her in a demeaning manner.

Zolah also saw the changes in the way Ham treated his wife and recognized them for what they were. Unable to watch any longer without saying something, she finally went to Ophea and sat her down with the intention of trying to help her sister-in-law deal with this growing problem.

"You must not allow him to do this," Zolah insisted. "You're just letting him walk all over you, Ophea. If you don't stand up for yourself, the problem will only get worse." Zolah rubbed Ophea's hands as she spoke, trying to get her sister-in-law to listen and understand the importance of what she was saying.

"I—I can't," answered Ophea. "You don't understand, Zolah."

"Ha! You think I don't?" Zolah's anger toward Ham was rising, along with her frustration with Ophea's apparent unwillingness to help herself. "I most certainly do understand! And by the way, if you're thinking that any of this is your fault, then you'd best think again."

But no matter how hard Zolah tried to reason with her, Ophea simply turned a deaf ear to her sister-in-law's earnest entreaties. Then, one overcast day when the wind outside of the ark was whipping the water into foam-crested waves, something happened that dramatically changed Ophea's poor opinion of herself. Indeed, it served as a revelation to everyone on the ark, including Ham.

It all started when Ham was heading toward the hold with a heavy load of freshly cut planks balanced over one shoulder and a hammer in his left hand. Just as he approached the top of the ladder, a gust of heavy wind hit the side of the ark. The jolt to the vessel was just enough to cause Ham to lose his grip on the handrail. Dropping the load of wood and flailing with his arms to regain his balance, Ham went crashing over the side of the ladder. He landed with a sickening thud on the deck below.

The fall caused a bad break to the bones of his right forearm, but that was not the worst of his injuries. Several of the wooden planks had splintered when they'd fallen onto the lower deck. Ham landed with tremendous force directly on top of the splintered boards. Unfortunately, one of the jagged pieces became impaled in the calf of his left leg, boring all the way to the bone. His sudden cries of pain brought the entire family at a run.

Naamah took one look at the wide gash with the protruding splinter of wood and knew that the injury was very serious indeed. The broken bones in Ham's arm might knit, but the wound to his leg was cause for great concern because of the danger of infection. This had always been one of Naamah's worst fears, for while she knew the basics of treating illnesses and injuries, she had no expertise in the art of healing when it came to infections. In the past, she had often turned to Rhema for help in treating wounds, for the younger woman had a way with the sick and injured animals. But this time it was obvious that Ham's injuries were more than even Rhema could handle.

Trying to lift Ham's head so she could comfort her son, Naamah was quickly brushed aside by Ophea. Cradling her husband's head in her lap, Ophea began to croon to him as a mother would comfort a hurt child. By then, Ham's teeth were chattering, and he was trembling all over from the shock. Noah pulled off his long cloak and covered his injured son.

"We'll have to splint his arm and pull that chunk of wood out of his leg before we can move him," said Shem. He looked around at the others, hoping that someone else was brave enough to handle the task. Only small rivulets of blood were seeping from the edges of the leg wound now, but Shem knew that as soon as they tried to extract the jagged dagger of wood, the bleeding would be profuse. He had always been squeamish at the sight of blood, and his stomach began to churn with just the thought of it.

Ophea lifted her head and looked around at the circle of worried faces. Suddenly, with a voice filled with a command that none of them had ever heard before, she began to bark out orders. **"Zolah!"** she shouted. "Get a large pot of water boiling. Make sure there are plenty of hot coals in the fire."

She turned around to assess the assembled company. "Rhema," she said, "You go to the storage area and find some strips of cloth. Make sure you get a good supply—and, Rhema, make absolutely sure that they are clean!"

Without questioning Ophea's newfound authority, the two women clambered up the ladder to do as they'd been told.

Gritting his teeth with pain, Ham managed to lift himself up enough so he could inspect the wound. "It's got to be cauterized," he said through his clenched teeth. Sweat poured from his forehead and dripped onto his beard. He grasped at the thigh of his left leg and squeezed it tightly as his face turned ashen with pain. He tried his best to remain calm.

Naamah dropped down next to Ophea. "What should I do?" she asked. She too was trying to stay calm, but she dreaded the thought of what must come next.

Ophea gave Naamah a weak smile, then turned once more to her injured husband. "Yes, my love," she answered, "we will have to cauterize the wound, but you'll be all right because you're strong, and you heal fast." She leaned over and used the hem of her shift to wipe the sweat from Ham's brow.

Ham used his good left hand to grasp Shem's arm. "Get it over with!" he gasped. "Just get it over with as fast as you can."

Japheth had already gone up the ladder and run to the kitchen area. Placing an iron bar into the hot coals of the fire, he added more wood and used a bellows to fan the flames. Ophea might know how to bandage a wound and set a broken arm, but cauterizing a gash like that was man's work!

In the meantime, Rhema had climbed back down the ladder with a bundle of clean strips of cloth. Minutes later, Zolah stood at the top of the ladder asking for someone to help her with the pot of boiling water. It took Japheth longer to arrive with the iron bar, its heated end glowing fiery red.

"Father Noah. Shem. Do you think you can hold him down firmly enough?" asked Ophea.

Without another word, they went to work. Ophea placed a smooth stick in Ham's mouth and told him to bite down hard on it. Poor Ham tried his best to be brave, but when Ophea yanked out the splinter of wood and Japheth pressed the glowing end of the iron bar against the gushing wound, he let out a blood-curdling scream. The smell of burning flesh filled the air.

Ophea waited for her husband to quiet down before she went to work setting his right forearm. It was a difficult job because the broken bones of the forearm were out of alignment, and his hand was already starting to swell. By the time she had stretched the arm enough to re-align the broken ends of the bones, dark bruises were beginning to form from Ham's elbow all the way down to his wrist.

"As soon as I've finished setting your arm, my love," said Ophea, "I'll see what I can do about making a salve to soothe the burning pain on your leg. I know it hurts something fierce right now, Ham, but it will heal. I promise you it will heal."

Ham could only nod as he gripped his wife's hands and made hard hissing noises through his clenched teeth. The pain was excruciating, but as he looked into Ophea's worried face, he recognized both a new beauty and a great strength that he had never seen before. "You're amazing," he whispered. "Truly amazing!"

Ophea smiled through her tears and bent down to kiss Ham's lips. "So are you," she said. "What's more, you're very brave."

For the first few days, the cauterized wound on Ham's leg appeared to be healing well, but Ophea was worried. She did not like the look of the skin around the edges of the wound. On the fifth day as the burned area began to fester, Ophea knew that she must change her method of treatment. She went to Naamah and asked if she could look through the various dried herbs that were stored in the small room just off the kitchen area.

Ophea took some time going through the various dried herbs, but was not completely satisfied with what she found. "Naamah," she asked, "I know you love flowers. Is there any chance that you might have stored away some roots or bulbs from your garden or from the meadow that lay in front of your home?"

Naamah's smile was like a ray of bright sunshine. "You've found me out, Ophea," she said in a hushed voice. She put her finger against her lips as she pulled Ophea into a dark corner of the storage room. "Now don't tell Father Noah, because he was quite insistent that we only had room to store things that we would absolutely need for food or medicine. If he knew that I've hidden away some of the roots, bulbs and seeds of my favorite flowers, he might question my lack of faith."

She rummaged around, moving sacks of this and that aside. Finally, she pulled out a large box that she'd carefully hidden under some heavy bags of dried wheat. When Naamah opened the box,

Ophea was pleased to see a large assortment of packets containing seeds, roots and flower bulbs, each carefully marked to indicate its content.

"Oh, Mother Naamah, this is wonderful!" she exclaimed. "Now I'm praying that you've managed to save the roots of some wild irises; you know, the beautiful purple and blue ones that grew along the edges of the meadow."

Naamah's eyes fairly sparkled. "Why, yes," she said in a conspiratorial whisper. "Those are some of my very favorite flowers. Here, let me see if I can find them." Riffling through the various pouches, Naamah finally found what she was looking for.

"Here they are," she said. "But, Ophea, what do you need wild iris roots for?"

Ophea grasped the package against her breast. "Mother Naamah, I hope you don't mind, but I may have to use up all of these roots. I know how you're hoping to plant these in the garden you'll have when we're out of this ark, but isn't saving Ham's leg far more important than growing flowers?"

Naamah looked perplexed. "Well, of course, child! But, Ophea, I don't understand. How will those few iris roots save Ham's leg?"

Ophea began to open the bag to inspect the viability of the roots. "Because, Mother, Ham's wound is becoming badly inflamed, and I'm very afraid that the infection may spread. I intend to grind these roots to powder and then make a poultice. It's the best thing I know to cure infected wounds."

Naamah grasped Ophea's arm and looked deeply into her eyes. "Daughter, how did you come by this knowledge of healing? Who taught you, and why have you not said anything about it before?"

Ophea's eyes clouded over. She dropped her head and scuffed her fingers in the dust on the floor. "I know I should have told you, Mother Naamah, but I was afraid—and—and terribly ashamed."

"Ashamed? Why should you be ashamed of having such an important and useful knowledge?"

Ophea was quiet for some time. Naamah watched in amazement as the younger woman's chin began to quiver and large teardrops fell from the lower lids of her eyes. Suddenly, Ophea was crying as though her heart were breaking. She tried to control her emotions, but she could only manage a few quick gulps before the torrent of tears began again. Naamh pulled Ophea against her breast and rubbed her hands along the younger woman's heaving back.

"What is it, child? Why are you so wracked with grief?"

Ophea swiped at her nose and tried to scrub the tears from her eyes. "Because, Naamah, I could have saved them! If only I'd been there, I could have saved them!"

"Saved who?" asked Naamah, totally perplexed by her daughter-in-law's outburst. And then, suddenly, she understood. "Your parents!" she whispered. "You think you could have saved your parents, is that it?"

"Yes," Ophea sniffled loudly and again swiped at her noise and eyes. "If only I had been there. You see my grandmother was a healer. She learned the art from her mother and taught it to me. She knew so much about the roots, herbs and plants used to heal all kinds of illnesses. People came from miles around, seeking her out, pleading with her for healing. She knew how to treat the most grievous wounds. I spent a great deal of time with her, Naamah, and when she died, people would come to me for help."

"And you never told us of this?" asked Naamah, in shocked amazement. "Why? What were you afraid of?"

"It wasn't that I was afraid—oh, no, never that!" Ophea had managed to control her tears now, but her face was as white as the flakes of snow that they had seen just days ago. She dropped her head and pressed her face into her hands. "It's all my fault! They shouldn't have died! If I had just been there, I could have saved them." She lifted her head again and looked into Naamah's eyes. Then, with a heart-wrenching sob, she grasped her mother-in-law's shoulders for support. "Oh, Naamah, I loved them so! I didn't want them to die, not that way!"

"But, Ophea," gasped Naamah, "you can't blame yourself for what happened. If you had been there- - -."

Ophea pressed a hand against Naamah's lips, stopping her in mid-sentence. "No, you don't understand. I **could** have saved them, Naamah. Yes, their wounds were severe, but not life threatening. If someone had stopped the bleeding. . . . But no, they just lay there for hours and slowly bled to death. And—and, oh Naamah, I could have saved them!"

By now, Naamah's own tears were flowing freely. She wrapped her arms around her daughter-in-law and tried to comfort her. "Oh, my poor child," she said. "All this time you've been holding in these feelings of guilt and remorse. I could never quite understand why you didn't mourn for your parents, but now I do. Now I understand."

Holding Ophea away so she could look her in the eye, Naamah's voice became very serious. "Listen to me, daughter. The fact that you weren't there is **not** your fault. You had no way of knowing what was happening—or even what was about to happen. And if you had been there, Ophea, those murdering villains might have killed you, too. You are **not** responsible for the deaths of your parents!"

Once again, Naamah pulled Ophea close. "I am so sorry that you had to go through this. But what is happening now—please understand me—what is happening now is truly good. You're finally able to grieve for them, Ophea. When we lose those whom we love, we need time to mourn them. You never had that time—at least not until now. You wouldn't allow yourself to grieve because you carried such a heavy weight of guilt. But the guilt is not yours, my child. It is **not** yours! Learn to forgive yourself, even as God has forgiven you. Mourn the loss of your parents, but then, try to remember all of the times of joy you had with them. Remember what they've given to you: your strength of character, your faith, your ability to love, your gentle spirit. Those are the things of importance, Ophea, and you have them in great measure."

And so it was that Ophea began to blossom into a woman of strength, one who was no longer afraid to express her emotions, for now she was an integral part of the only family on earth to have survived the Great Flood.

Chapter Eight

The Waiting Time

God, the one and only—I'll wait as long as he says.
Everything I hope for comes from him, so why not?
He's rock under my feet, breathing room for my soul,
An impregnable castle: I'm set for life. My help and glory
are in God—granite strength and safe-harbor God—
So trust him absolutely, people, lay your lives on the line for him.
God is a safe place to be. Psalms 62:5-8

A delicious aroma drifted from Naamah's kitchen. Like a beckoning finger, the rich smell of a fig cake fresh from the oven enticed the entire family to drop what they were doing and quickly make their way to their living quarters. Shem, Ham and Japheth were the first to arrive, followed closely by their wives, and eventually Noah. "Ah-ha!" exclaimed Naamah as she turned to see them standing expectantly in the doorway. "I knew the smell of this cake would capture your attention."

It had been more than a month since Naamah had prepared their favorite dessert, and short of a miracle, this would probably be the last fig cake they would enjoy for a very long time. Their supply of dried figs was growing low, and the precious lal,[16] a honey-like substance extracted from the sap of a date palm tree that Naamah preferred to use as a sweetener for her fig cake, was quickly disappearing.

Naamah had been saving the last of the lal for a special occasion. Noah's birthday was coming up in a few weeks, an event that she hoped to celebrate in style. She had done her best to apportion out the dwindling ingredients in the hope that they would last, but now it was not to be, for Naamah saw a crisis in the making—one that might possibly be averted if she could get everyone's cooperation. The trick, of course, was to put the family in a good mood, and nothing did that faster than her fig cakes.

Over the past few weeks, Naamah had become increasingly aware of a dangerous lethargy that had come over her family. Noah was the only one who seemed to maintain a lively interest in the day-to-day activities. The others were growing bored and seemed to be constantly getting on each other's nerves. Angry outbursts and disruptive arguments occurred with ever-growing frequency, often over the most insignificant matters. Family meal times, which in the past had been filled with laughter and convivial conversation, were quickly deteriorating into sullen and silent events.

Naamah had observed these changes with growing apprehension, and after considering the problem, she began to realize that some creative solutions were needed. If her husband could remain cheerful and mentally active, why couldn't the others do likewise? What was it that kept him so alert? How was he occupying his free time?

It hadn't take Naamah long to discover the reasons for her husband's lack of boredom. While her sons and daughters-in-law spent their free time moping about with little more to look forward to than eventually getting out of the ark, her husband kept himself busy with a project that was both creative and challenging.

Noah was writing the story of the world before the flood. He had already completed the account of Adam and Eve's sojourn in the Garden of Eden, their temptation and fall, their expulsion, and the tragic story of their sons, Cain and Abel. At the present he was recording stories from the lives of those godly men who were the descendents of Adam and Eve, carefully tracing the ten generations that included spiritual giants like Enoch, Methusalah and his own father, Lamech.

Just two nights ago, Naamah had sat next to her husband watching him scratch out the words with a stylus that he dipped into an inky substance made from powdered charcoal mixed with small amounts of olive oil. His tablets consisted of thin pieces of rawhide stretched tightly over wooden frames. She recalled the words he spoke to her that night and sensed that this would become a work of great importance. Noah was writing, not only the history of his lineage, but also the culture and the values which had existed before this great deluge. In her heart, Naamah felt certain that, in generations to come, others would value these vital records.

"As soon as we are out of the ark," he had said, "I will have to prepare some clay tablets and copy this information so it will be more permanent. The writing on these makeshift scraps of rawhide works well for now, but it will fade quickly. Perhaps I can get the boys to help me."

Naamah was pleased to hear that Noah wanted to involve his sons in this important work. "Oh, yes," she answered. "It is right that you put down everything, even those things that are painful to record, for how else will those who come after us understand how and why we came to this time and place. But, Noah, will they believe, or will they think they are just fanciful stories?"

"Some will believe," said Noah. "And those who do will be blessed."

Noah pulled Naamah close to him and planted a kiss on her forehead. "There is still much to record," he said, "and not all of it is bad. But right now, Wife, my poor, old eyes are growing weary, and I feel the cold in my bones. Snuff out the lamps, my love, and let us go to bed where it's warm."

As Naamah lay beside her husband that night, she thought about what he was doing, and it was then that the realization came to her. But of course, this was what they all needed. Oh, not recording the past as Noah was doing, but something more than the tedious work of caring for the animals. They needed to find things to do that were creative—things that would make them want to finish up their chores so they could put their hands and minds to something more challenging.

And so it was that Naamah decided to use the last of her figs to make this delicious dessert. She spent most of the day preparing for the evening when they would all be together in their living quarters.

The Women of the Ark

She prepared a hearty meal consisting of a rich lentil soup, leeks and fresh beans that she had grown in her potted garden, two loaves of her delicious wheat bread, and a large tray filled with lovely, white chunks of goat cheese, dried fruits and a selection of nuts dipped in honey. The meal in itself would be sumptuous, but with the addition of her fig cake, it was sure to bring about a more convivial atmosphere.

The family members quickly found their seats and began to fill their bowls with Naamah's good lentil soup. They broke off large chunks of the wheat bread, using them to sop up the last bits of broth in the bottom of their bowls. Naamah covertly watched them as they helped themselves to large servings of the vegetables, cheese, dried fruits, and honeyed nuts. She could see that the lines on their faces were softening. Small smiles of pleasure pulled at the corners of their mouths, though there was still little conversation going on. Naamah waited until they had each finished their first slice of fig cake. Then, with contentment all around, she stood up, cleared her throat, and gently rapped her knuckles on the table.

"I am pleased that you have all enjoyed this good meal," she said, "especially my fig cake. I had thought to save the ingredients for a more auspicious occasion." At this, her eyes twinkled as she gave her husband a knowing look. "But in view of the fact that we no longer seem to be able to communicate with each other at meal times, I decided it would be best not to wait. As the women of this family know, it is becoming increasingly more difficult to come up with meals that offer some variation in our diet, and perhaps that has something to do with our lack of interest in mealtimes. Sadly, that same lethargy seems to have crept into other aspects of our time here on the ark. I've thought about this problem a lot lately, and have come to the conclusion that we need to find some other ways—creative ways—to put variety in our lives."

It was obvious that she had everyone's attention, for they were now all staring at her with looks that seemed to be a mix of contriteness and confusion. She had hoped that there would be no comments until after she had said her piece, but that was not to be, for Ham had quickly picked up on her reference to their dwindling food supplies.

Pushing himself away from the table, Ham let out a snort of disgust. "If our food provisions are growing that low, Mother, there's one certain way to take care of the problem and put variety in our diet at the same time." He scanned the faces around him, knowing that they all understood exactly what he meant.

"NO, Ham!" Noah's response was quick and decisive. "We are not going to start slaughtering the animals, not a single one of them! God did not place these creatures under our protection to have us killing and eating them. They are on this ark to preserve them so the earth might be replenished once this flood is over." He gave Ham a stern look. "You know that, my son. And you also know that God has not given us permission to eat the flesh of animals."

Next Japheth jumped into the fray, for he could not let this pronouncement pass without an argument. "Father, surely God does not want us to starve to death! What would be the harm if we killed just a few of the smaller fowls? It would give us extra nourishment and help vary our meals. Besides, there were many who ate the flesh of birds and animals before this flood. How can you be so certain that God does not expect us to do likewise now?"

Noah shook his head as he pounded the table with his fist. "I'll not listen to such talk—not from any of you! Japheth, Ham, you know that God has commanded that we care for these creatures with our very lives. If we cannot have enough faith to believe that He will provide for all of our needs, including the food we eat, then this entire voyage will have been made in vain."

"Oh, dear," said Naamah, "I never meant to start such a bitter conflict. I only wanted to point out that we must find ways to occupy our minds and hands in a more creative manner. Our food is not really the issue here—surely you see that." Wringing her hands in frustration, Naamah gave her husband a worried look.

Noah reached over and patted Naamah's hands. "It's all right my dear. Perhaps it is best that we cleared the air on this matter." He glanced from one to the other, then lowered his head and began tapping his fingers on the table. "I've prayed about it many times." Looking up at Naamah, and then at each of his sons in turn, Noah tried to explain what he felt God was telling him. "The time may well come when the Lord gives us permission to eat the flesh of animals," he said, his voice low and filled with earnest conviction.

"But while we are in this ark of safety, we must not succumb to the temptation to destroy what God has trusted us to protect."

Naamah shook her head in disbelief. How could all of her efforts have come to this? She had hoped to bring her family together by preparing them a good meal, and instead, it had lead to a bitter argument. But Naamah was not about to let her ideas be pushed aside—not now when the very bonds of her family's unity were at stake.

"Ham, Japheth," she said, her voice now strong and demanding attention, "your father is right, and you both know it, but food is not the issue here. I am sorry if I mislead you by mentioning our reduced supply of dried figs. I certainly had not intended to start such an unpleasant argument, but the fact that it occurred is further proof that my concerns are well-founded."

"Mother!" Ham exclaimed. "You have been too long in this ark! Exactly what is it you expect us to do? Shall we start weaving the hay into garlands? Or perhaps we can teach that bull elephant that is fond of throwing people about to stand on his hind legs and dance." With a snort of disgust, he pushed himself back from the table.

Naamah narrowed her eyes and gave her youngest son a reprimanding look. "Don't be impertinent, Ham!" she scolded. "You know perfectly well what I mean. We need to find ways to expand our minds. We need to find things to do that will make our days less tiresome."

"The only thing that will make my days less tiresome," retorted Ham, "is to get off this boat! I'm tired of being confined like this. I'm tired of seeing nothing but water when I look out the window." With that, he pushed himself up, and stalked away. Sheepishly, the other men also stood and went off to start their daily chores, leaving the women seated there by themselves.

Ophea dropped her head and let out a deep sigh. "I'm sorry, Mother Naamah," she said. "I don't know what's gotten into Ham lately. He's always so angry. No matter what I do or say, I can't seem to please him."

Rhema stood up and began to pace around the table. Then suddenly, she turned and clapped her hands together to get their attention. "Mother Naamah is right," she said. "It's high time we stopped moping about and thought of something that will make the days go faster." Glancing down to the floor, she spotted the dried peel of a pomegranate that they had failed to sweep up. She plucked it up, held it in her hand, and began to examine it. Moving it from one hand to the other, a crease began to form between her eyes as she studied the deep, red color of the peel. Without another word, she turned and left the kitchen area, taking with her the dried bit of pomegranate skin.

The next morning, after the men had finished their breakfast and the four women were cleaning up the eating area, Rhema reached into her pocket and pulled out a small leather packet. With great care, she untied the string that held it together. Smiling at the others who had now grown curious, she went to the table and spilled out a tiny mound of a dark, red powder. Holding up a finger and giving the other women a mischievous look, Rhema reached for a flask of water, dipped in her finger, then let a few droplets of water fall onto the red powder. Once again using the tip of her finger, she carefully mixed the water into the powder, then, with a chuckle she turned toward Zolah and swiped her finger straight down her sister-in-law's nose.

Ophea clapped her hands in delight. "Oh, Zolah," she laughed. "You should see yourself!"

Zolah screwed up her face, crossed her eyes, and tried to look down at her nose. "What? Is there something wrong?"

Naamah chuckled as she examined her daughter-in-law's face. "Why, you have a lovely, red streak right down the center of your nose, my dear," she said. Reaching out she touched her finger to the tip of Zolah's nose as she tried to control her laughter, for poor Zolah was looking quite disconcerted.

"Is that so!" exclaimed Zolah. "Well, I suppose I should return the favor." She dashed the tip of her finger into the small puddle of red dye that was now seeping into the wooden planks of the table, then quickly turned and swiped it across Rhema's forehead.

Within seconds, the three younger women were giggling like children as they bounced around the table and marked each other's faces with the red dye. Abandoning all propriety, Naamah joined in the hilarity. How good it felt to laugh and simply let herself go! When had she last done anything like this? Quite honestly, she couldn't remember.

"Whew!" exclaimed Naamah, when she was finally able to catch her breath, "If Father Noah had walked in here while **that** was going on, he would have been quite certain that we'd all lost our minds! But to tell you the truth, there's nothing like a good laugh to make one feel about thirty years younger." She gave the three young women a conspiratorial smile, then patted her hair into place and straightened out her apron. "Actually," she said, trying to make her voice sound serious, "painting each others faces wasn't exactly what I was thinking of when I said we needed to expand our minds, but I guess it's as good a start as any."

Rhema wiped the tears of laughter from her eyes. "It's a wonderful start!" she exclaimed as she fished around in the deep pocket of her shift. "Look," she said as she pulled out two more leather pouches, "I must show you some of the other colors I've come up with. I've been trying a little of this and a little of that." She cleared an area on the table in front of her and reached for several small bowls. "Mother Naamah, do you remember how you once used different plants and vegetables to make dyes for the wool that you would spin into yarn?"

"Yes," answered Naamah, "but I was never very good at it. The colors were not bright enough for my taste, and they faded so quickly."

Rhema nodded her head, "Ah, but at least you tried." She carefully opened one of the pouches. "The problem, of course, was that you simply didn't have the time to really work at it, neither did you have a background of knowledge. Dying yarn and cloth is an art. It takes time and effort to discover what works best. And there's also the process needed to set the dyes so they don't fade."

Zolah pulled her stool a little closer. "And how do you know so much about this, Rhema?" she asked. "I've never heard you mention anything about this before."

Asking for patience, Rhema lifted a finger, then carefully poured a small amount of yellow powder into one of the shallow bowls. "When I was a child, I had an uncle who owned a large workshop in the village near where we lived. He had several artisans working for him, men who knew not only how to create lovely colors of dye, but also how to weave the finest yarns and threads into beautiful fabrics.

My uncle was a very wealthy man with a reputation for carrying nothing but the best of goods. Merchants and traders would come from all over to purchase his materials. But for me, the best place of was the yard behind the workshop. That's where they dyed the yarn in large vats that sat over the fire braziers. Then they would hang up the drying yarn from ropes attached to very high poles." Rhema heaved a great sigh of pleasure. "Oh, when I close my eyes," she said, "I can still see all those long strings of colored yarn looped over the ropes, blowing in the wind. What a picture they made!"

Stopping to catch her breath, Rhema opened another bag and spilled its contents into a bowl. This time, the powder was a light shade of blue. "And I loved to watch the workmen stirring those big pots of dye. Sometimes, the dye would spill over the sides of the vat and dribble down onto the ground, leaving the most wonderful puddles of color. Of course, eventually the puddles would dry up, but the sandy soil would retain some of the color." She smiled as the memories came flooding back. "After the shop was closed," she said, "I'd sneak in the back and fill my pockets with all of that beautifully colored sand."

By then the other women were staring at Rhema in fascination. They could picture exactly what she was talking about. The world that they had known before the flood had indeed been filled with sin and violence, but it had also contained much beauty. How they longed for the day when they would once more be able to see such wonderful sights!

Turning to face her mother-in-law, Rhema clasped her hands together and pressed her chin against her knuckles. "Do you remember how lovely your bolt of cloth was, Mother Naamah?" she asked, "The one that you ended up throwing to the mob when we were trying to enter the ark?"

Naamah nodded. "How could I ever forget that? Even now it gives me the shivers just to think of it."

"Well," continued Rhema, "whoever made that cloth or the threads woven into it surely knew how to produce beautifully colored dyes that did not fade over time. It was an exquisite piece of workmanship!" She hesitated for a moment as her eyes took on a faraway look. "Do you know, I can't get it off my mind that that piece of fabric may well have come from my uncle's shop."

"Oh, my!" exclaimed Naamah. "Could it be?"

Rhema shrugged her shoulders. "I suppose it's possible, but we'll never know, will we? For the workmen who made it are certainly dead. And sadly, all of their know-how went with them."

It was a sobering thought, one which caused the women to lapse into a deep silence as their minds drifted back to the violent storms and upheavals that had brought on this world-wide flood. Surely, the only creatures that could still be alive outside of this ark would be those who were naturally the inhabitants of a watery world. What sort of an earth would they find when they were at last free from their lengthy confinement? How would they survive if even the earth's vegetation had been destroyed? Thinking more seriously of this than she had dared do before, Naamah determined that she must share these emerging fears with her husband, but her worrisome thoughts were interrupted by her daughter-in-law's next remark.

"The point is," said Rhema, "that cloth was made by craftsmen who were very talented and knew a lot about creating bright and colorful dyes. And while it likely took them years, if not generations to learn the secrets of their trade, we have to start somewhere if we are ever to learn how it was done. So, why not make that start right here on the ark. Considering the fact that we have so much time on our hands, it would be a wonderful activity that we can all get involved in—that is, all of us who are interested."

Suddenly, Zolah clasped her hands together as she let out a shout of glee. "Oh, Rhema, wouldn't it be wonderful if we could discover their secrets!"

Rhema smiled at Zolah's remark, then a look of determination came over her face. "And so we shall!" she said, her voice rising with excitement. "Oh, I don't expect to discover everything immediately, especially as confined as we are. But I've already managed to come up with these three colors. And just wait until you see what else I've thought of." She stood up, flung her arms wide then walked over to one of the partitions. She rubbed her hands along the textured surface of the dried rawhide. "I'm going to start by painting all kinds of wonderful scenes on these partitions," she said as she pointed to the wall partitions that had been made by stretching large sheets of partially treated leather over wooden frames. "Forests with tall trees and fields filled with flowers! Houses and sparkling, blue lakes! Oh, you're just going to love this room by the time I'm finished decorating it!"

Ophea could barely control her excitement now. "Oh, please Rhema, may I help?" She rushed over to a wide shelf that held a line of clay jugs. "Do you think I could paint some designs on our pottery? And what about these bowls?" she asked. "Wouldn't they look lovely if they were decorated with bright colors?"

"I can just see them now," answered Rhema. "Of course, for pottery, you might need to use more of a paste than this watery dye, but that should be easy enough to make."

Pushing her stool back so she could lean her shoulders and head against the wall, Naamah smiled to herself as she watched her daughters-in-law chatter together about their newly made plans. "Yes!" she said to herself. "This is exactly what is needed. Now, if I can only get my sons equally involved in some interesting projects."

Rhema was true to her word. Over the next several weeks, she worked feverishly at creating all kinds of lovely dyes and paints. She mixed one color with another, darkening some by adding a little of the blackened powder from burnt firewood, lightening others by diluting them with water or small amounts of their precious nectars. She experimented with their stores of roots and vegetables, scraped off bits of the lichens and mosses that were growing along the wooden frames of the long window. And to the utter disgust of her husband, she even created dyes using blood and urine.

Before long, many of the leather partitions in the family's living quarters were vibrant with all sorts of colorful scenes and landscapes. In a way, walking past one of Rhema's painted partitions was like once more walking upon dry land. There were wide vistas and lovely scenes of gardens filled with flowers, lush woodlands, meadows bright with sunshine, and here and there, some soft, blue lakes with their waters well confined within distinct shorelines. Rhema had added her favorite creatures to the scenes, mostly horses, but sometimes zebras, antelopes and gazelles. Very rarely did she paint the human form, for she found it difficult to think of the earth being once again filled with people who did not appreciate the beauty that surrounded them.

Ophea's interest in decorating their many clay pots and pieces of pottery blossomed into a project that kept a smile on her face throughout much of the day. Only in the evenings when her increasingly more sullen husband belittled her efforts and ridiculed her artwork did she sink back into a dejected silence.

Ham's face was now so often filled with anger and resentment that Naamah shuddered to think of what might happen if someone dared to cross him. He was like a seething volcano that could erupt at any moment. She found herself tiptoeing around him whenever he entered her kitchen. How could this be, she wondered? How could she actually have come to the point where she dreaded to be near her dearly beloved, youngest son?

To make matters worse, Naamah was greatly worried about Ophea, for she was beginning to suspect that the young woman might be pregnant. Of course, for many years Naamah had longed for the birth of a grandchild. She understood that God, in His infinite mercy and wisdom, had surely delayed such a thing from happening in view of the traumatic events they had endured before the flood. But now, perhaps the time was right. Surely it wouldn't be too much longer before their confinement in the ark would end. Then, the earth would have to be repopulated. Only her sons and daughters-in-law could fulfill that need. Still, Naamah's growing concerns often kept her awake at night, for Ham's truculent behavior did not bode well for the safety of his wife, let alone a defenseless child.

Thankfully, Japheth and Shem were still a joy to be around. They had taken a great interest in the artistic endeavors of the women. Periodically, they would stop in front of one of the beautifully decorated partitions and gaze wistfully at the lovely scenes. When they sat down to eat a meal, they often praised Ophea's creative designs painted on the outside of their bowls. Even Zolah, who was generally considered to be somewhat lacking when it came to creating artwork with Rhema's paints and dyes, received her fair share of appreciation from Shem and Japheth. In fact, Zolah was involved in one small incident that had them all entertained for several days.

It happened when Zolah decided that she had no interest in trying to paint landscapes on leather or geometric designs on pottery. Always a bit more eccentric than the others, Zolah preferred to make odd shapes and patterns that only she seemed to recognize as having any meaning. At times, she simply created great splashes of color that, to the others, appeared to be the haphazard wanderings of a confused mind. But Naamah never criticized her efforts, for Zolah seemed to be enjoying herself, and that was, in itself, valuable.

Neither did it matter what sort of surface Zolah painted on. One day, when Japheth entered the elephants' cage, the one that held the same bull who had enjoyed tossing people about with his powerful trunk, he was shocked to see a tracing of colorful, squiggly lines and shapes painted on the broad expanse of the mammoth's right side.

"ZOLAH!" he shouted, for he immediately knew who had done this deed. When Zolah peered around the corner of the cage door, her face a mask of innocence, but her eyes gleaming with mischief, he began to berate her in no uncertain terms.

"WHAT DO YOU THINK YOU'RE DOING IN HERE, AND ALL BY YOURSELF!" shouted Japheth.

Zolah simply shrugged her shoulders, lifted her eyes toward the ceiling, and began to hum a little tune. There was a smear of blue paint on her right cheek and several spots of red paint on her chin. She twiddled her thumbs then gave poor Japheth a beguiling grin.

"Don't you know that this great beast could have injured you severely if he stomped you with his foot?" asked Japheth. "Or what if he had chosen to simply roll over on you while you were busily painting his side?"

Zolah began to giggle. "I guess he'd have squashed me flat," she said, trying to control her urge to laugh out loud.

"ZOLAH, THIS IS NOT A LAUGHING MATTER!" shouted Japheth.

"But, Japheth," she said, her voice now as sweet as honey, "this poor old fellow may be big, but he's really quite a sweetheart. In fact, he and I have become the best of friends. You see, I always slip him some special treats from the kitchen."

Zolah walked over and patted the bull elephant's side in a most familiar manner. "Besides, Japheth, he **liked** having his side painted.

Actually, I think that the feel of the brush going up and down his skin was probably very relaxing. Look at his eyes, Japheth." She nimbly climbed up onto the edge of the feed trough and tugged at the end of the creature's flopping ear. "Now you see, doesn't he look happy?" she asked.

Japheth hit his forehead with the heel of his hand, then grasped Zolah's shoulders, spun her around, and shoved her out of the cage. "I intend to tell Shem about your foolish behavior," he said, as stern lines formed around the corners of his mouth and eyes. "We'll just see how amused he is by this lack of concern you have for your own safety!"

But later that day, when Japheth happened to see his brother Shem walk past on his way to one of the storage bins, he had to stop short and let out a gasp of surprise. Shem turned around to look Japheth squarely in the eye. Sure enough, there on Shem's right cheek were the same squiggly lines painted in the very same colors that Zolah had created on the bull elephant's rump—only, of course, a much smaller version.

Chapter Nine

A Raven and a Dove

*He sent out a raven; it flew back and forth waiting
for the flood waters to dry up. Then he sent a dove to check
on the flood conditions, but it couldn't even find a place to perch—
water still covered the Earth. Noah reached out and caught it,
brought it back into the ship. He waited seven more days
and sent out the dove again. It came back in the evening with a
freshly picked olive leaf in its beak. Noah knew that
the flood was about finished. Genesis 8:7-11*

A thin, crescent moon hung like a silver bowl over the western horizon. One by one, stars began to fill the darkening sky with brilliant points of light. Naamah leaned as far out of the window as she could as she scanned the surface of the ever-moving flood. She thrilled to the knowledge that the waters that surrounded them teemed with life.

Just this morning she had watched in wonder as a great school of silvery fish approached the ark, turned en masse, then disappeared beneath the hull. A small pod of dolphin had been following their vessel's meandering course for several days, their friendly smiles and gentle eyes creating a feeling that something wonderful was soon to happen. She had seen the gray backs and the geyser-like water spouts of whales traveling along the horizon.

The Women of the Ark

Three days ago Japheth had managed to catch a very large sea turtle that had paddled close to the great vessel. Hoping to pull the creature up through the high window, he had called his brothers to come help him. "Just imagine what a tasty meal this fellow will make," he'd said. "A little tough, perhaps, but certainly nourishing, and I remember someone telling me once that turtle flesh makes a delicious soup."

Shem and Ham evidently liked the idea, for they put their backs into it and began to haul the massive creature up the side of the ark. The hapless turtle beat its flippers frantically against the wooden sideboards, sending a reverberating thumping sound throughout the vessel. But just when the three brothers felt certain that they had won the battle, the turtle twisted its massive head upward, grasped hold of the hemp rope that had ensnared him, and using his sharp beak, managed to bite it in half. Freed from his would-be captures, he fell back into the water with a loud splash and quickly disappeared into the dark sea.

Naamah smiled at the memory of this incident. She was quite pleased that she had not been called upon to make turtle soup. Indeed, it gave her an even greater thrill to think of that wonderful creature swimming free somewhere out there beyond the horizon. She sniffed at the night air, enjoying the salty smell of it, thinking that this was what the turtle was also smelling. Then she stopped, held her breath, and took a very deep gulp of air.

What was that strange odor? Was it coming from outside the ark? She took another deep breath. Yes, there was something different in the air. Could it be the smell of the earth? Was there dry land somewhere out there? She cupped her hands around her eyes and searched the horizon, hoping to see something projecting into the sky. If only the moon were brighter. She thought she could see low clouds on the horizon, but what if they weren't clouds? Or perhaps they were clouds swirling around a mountain peak.

Naamah had an urge to call out to the others to come and help her look. But no, that would be foolish. They would only laugh at her, or worse yet, be angry for waking them up. How late was it, she wondered? Perhaps Noah was still awake. And even if he wasn't, he would understand.

The Women of the Ark

Deciding to wait just a little longer before going for her husband, she tried to tune all of her senses to the outside world. Then she heard a sound from within the ark. It was low and steady. Turning around, she listened intently. It was coming from somewhere beneath her. She went to the ladder and peered over the edge of the deck. It was so dark in the ark that she could see little more than shadows, but they were moving. The sound, she realized, was coming from the pens just below the deck that she was standing on.

Naamah leaned on the rail and tried to picture the creatures that were housed in the pens in this area. Ah, but of course, they were the large, hoofed animals—the caribou, water buffalos, bison, and elks. Curious as to what was happening beneath her, Naamah went back toward the window to pick up the oil lamp that she'd left on the floor. Moving quietly so as not to frighten the animals, she crept over to the top of the ladder, placed her feet on the upper rung, and began to climb down. When she was halfway down, she held up her lamp to illuminate the pens.

The flickering light of the oil lamp cast long shadows on the back wall of the pens. The shadows appeared to be swaying back and forth, back and forth. She pressed her arm against the side of the ladder, thinking that it was the lamp that was swaying in her hand. But no, the lamplight held steady. It was the animals themselves who were swaying. Their heads were tilted up with their noses pointing toward the decking above them, their nostrils flared outward. And then it struck her. The animals were sniffing the same strange odor that she had smelled when she was looking out the window. But of course! It was land! They too had caught the smell of dry land!

Forgetting her age, ignoring decorum, Naamah took the last rungs of the ladder in a series of hops then raced toward their living quarters. "UP!" she shouted as she ran down the long corridor. "EVERYONE UP! IT'S OUT THERE! I CAN SMELL IT! THE ANIMALS CAN SMELL IT!"

Her family came tumbling out of their sleeping compartments with bewildered looks on their faces and startled expressions in their eyes. Ignoring the fact that they were only half dressed and were looking at her as though she had gone mad, Naamah flapped her arms in the air and danced in circles around them. "LOOK UP

THERE!" she shouted. "LOOK AT THOSE BUFFALO. DO YOU SEE THEM SNIFFING AT THE AIR?"

Shem reached out and grasped Naamah around her middle, pinning her arms to her sides. "MOTHER, CALM YOURSELF!" he shouted as he tried to keep her from bouncing up and down.

Startled by Naamah's strange behavior, Zolah reached out and laid her hands gently on either side of her mother-in-law's face. "Mother," she said, trying to keep her voice steady "It's all right. You probably just had a bad dream." She turned to give her husband a worried look. "Oh, dear," she said. "Could she have been walking in her sleep? What if she'd fallen down the ladder?" Wrapping an arm around Naamah's shoulders, Zolah tried to pull her down onto a nearby bench. "Here, Mother," she said solicitously. "Sit down and rest a moment. You'll be all right in a minute or two."

Freed from Shem's tight hold, Naamah clapped her hands together and let out a hearty laugh. Then, glancing at her husband's worried face, she sat down and tried to put on a more sober expression. She let out a deep sigh, then, unable to control herself any longer, she let out another laugh as she clapped her hands with excitement. "Listen to me," she said as smile wrinkles radiated out from the corners of her eyes. I am not demented, nor have I been dreaming. And I can assure you, I have **not** been sleepwalking."

Noah sat down beside her and began to gently stroke her arms. "Well then, my love, tell us what's on your mind," he said with such serious tones that Naamah had all she could do not to laugh out loud.

Stifling the laugh that threatened to come bubbling out of her mouth, Naamah patted Noah's knees. "Husband," she said, "I want you to go over there and climb up that ladder. When you reach the upper deck, go to the window and take in a very deep breath. Then come back down here and tell us all exactly what you've smelled— besides water."

Everyone's head turned in unison to look up at the dim starlight coming through the high window. And then, almost tripping over each other in their race to reach the ladder, they clambered up to the narrow deck that ran just below the long window. With a knowing smile on her lips and her eyes alight, Naamah followed them.

The Women of the Ark

When she reached the upper deck, she saw that her entire family was standing on tip-toe as they leaned out the window and they sniffed at the air. Japheth was the first one to turn around. "I SMELL IT!" he shouted. "YOU'RE RIGHT, MOTHER! YOU ARE PERFECTLY RIGHT! THERE'S LAND OUT THERE! DRY LAND!" He reached Naamah in two long strides, grasped her outstretched hands and began to dance around with her. "LAND!" he shouted. "THERE'S LAND OUT THERE!"

Always the pessimist, Ham snorted and shook his head in disgust. "Well, as God is my witness," he said, "I don't smell a thing other than brackish water and damp air. I think the two of you must have cracks in your skulls."

Ophea turned from the window and grasped at her husband's wrist. "No, Ham," she said, her voice very quiet. "You're wrong. There is something different about the air. There's a musty smell to it, like the muddy ground at the edge of stream where I use to wade when I was a child."

Rhema joined them. "Yes," she said, "I too can smell it. I'm sure that Naamah is right. Somewhere out there in the night there is land, not dry land, perhaps, but muddy ground."

Noah pulled at his beard and tilted his head as though he were deep in thought. There was a moment of silence as he looked from one to the other. "Uh-huh," he said, as he smiled down at Naamah. "I do believe you're right, my dear. I should know better than to question you, for it seems you're generally right."

Naamah clasped her hands across her stomach and grinned at her sons and daughters-in-law. "You've heard your father," she intoned. "I'm right. In fact, I am **usually** right. Now climb down the ladder and go look at the animals in the pens just beneath this deck. Ham, you first. And when you get down there, tell me exactly what it is that they are doing—and why you think they are doing it."

She watched with smug satisfaction as her family clambered back down the ladder. Now that there were several oil lamps lighting the pens, it became obvious what the animals were doing. Indeed, by now they'd become quite excited, for not only were they sniffing at the air, they were also pawing at the flooring of their pens as though anxious to be let out.

Excitement rippled through the ark like flashes of distant lightening. Somewhere out there in the blackness of the night there was land exposed by the steadily dropping flood waters. It was far too dark to see it, but the smell of it was thrilling. After all of these long months of being confined in the ark, they would once again see the earth. And soon, they hoped—oh, very soon—the door of this great vessel would be opened and they would step out and know the glorious feeling of walking once again upon that good earth.

There was little sleep to be had that night, for humans and animals alike felt the rising tide of excitement and anticipation. When the morning came at last, Noah and his entire family were standing on the upper deck staring out the window and anxiously scanning the surface of the flood waters. Long before the sun crested the eastern horizon, even when the first gray light of early dawn touched the sky and sent shimmering waves of pale light across the surface of the sea, the small knot of people were straining their eyes in the hope of getting their first glimpse of a land mass. Wispy clouds blanketed the far reaches of the eastern sky, but as the bright globe of the sun crested the horizon, the gray sky slowly turned to a lavender-blue. As the sunlight touched the clouds, they began to glow first pink, then orange, then golden yellow. Wide rays of sunlight splayed out like an opening fan and shot upward into a sky that would soon be an azure blue. It was such a glorious sight that no one could speak. They could only stand there with their mouths open in wonder as tears of happiness streamed down their faces.

No land was seen that day, nor the next. But it didn't matter, for there could be no doubt that it was out there somewhere. What would it look like, this earth that had been torn and shattered by the cataclysmic events that had brought on the flood? Would they recognize anything at all? Would they see the broken remains of forests, homes and vineyards? Would there be anything left of the people and animals who had been drowned in the flood? These thoughts became more sobering with each passing day.

Noah set up a watch during the daylight hours, with each individual taking his or her turn to walk along the entire circumference of the upper deck and look out the window in a search for land. A

The Women of the Ark

week passed, then two, but still, there was nothing to be seen but water in every direction.

Then, when discouragement seemed to nip at everyone's heels, Japheth spotted the ragged top of a mountain peak sticking up out of the water. It was very distant, and because they had no means of navigating the ark, they could only stare at it longingly. Misty clouds hid it from sight each morning and evening, but as the sun grew warm during the daylight hours and burned off the clouds, the mountaintop would reappear like a blue mirage on the distant horizon.

As the days passed, the mountain peak grew ever larger. They could not tell for certain if they were just drifting nearer to it or if the receding flood waters were actually exposing more of it. Nevertheless, the sight of that jagged peak lifted everyone's spirits.

Then, the day came when the ark began to groan and shudder as its hull scrapped along something long and solid. The women held their breaths and pressed their hands to their mouths. The men raced for the ladders, pulling themselves up several rungs at a time. There was land under the ark, they were certain of it, but would it tear out the hull of their vessel? And if that were to happen, what could they do about it?

"Trust in God," said Noah, the man of great faith who had brought them to this time and place. "Trust in God, for He will not fail us or forsake us. He has brought us this far through tempests and floods, and He will see us through until we are once again on dry land."

And so it was that the ark began to settle into place at the very top of the hoary mountain peaks that would one day be known as the Ararat Range. A great wind arose and the waters continued to recede as the gale buffeted the vessel with such force that it shook to its very core. Its beams and boards creaked and groaned, but the well-built ark remained firmly wedged between the massive boulders that had been thrust up at the top of the mountain. The wind blew for forty days and nights as inch by inch, the floodwaters went down and more land was exposed. To those waiting on the ark, the ground beneath them appeared to be dry. Why then, had God not opened the massive door to let them out? Had He forgotten them? Would they remain imprisoned in this great vessel as they looked longingly out at a dry earth?

The Women of the Ark

Now even Noah was becoming anxious and his faith was strongly tested. If the door of the ark were suddenly opened, he wondered, would it be safe to leave? At this great elevation, they had no way of knowing what might lie beneath the clouds that encircled the mountain. In the distance, they could see many other peaks, but all of them were encased in a heavy cloud cover. And the air was growing colder. Surely they must leave this place soon, but would it be safe to try to make their way down the mountain? And if they did get out, would they find any food? They could see no trees or green vegetation. How would they get all of the animals down? The questions buzzed around in his head and left deep worry wrinkles on his brow.

Because of the heavy wind and the increasingly chilly air, they had tightly secured the protective flaps to cover the long window. Noah paced up and down along the upper deck, feeling the drafts of cold air that set his bones to aching. Finally, he decided that something must be done.

"Japheth," he called as he leaned over the railing to search for his eldest son. "Go to the cages where the birds are kept and fetch me a female raven. Make certain that she is healthy and strong, for I have an important task for her to perform." Noah wanted the female for she had young chicks in the nest and he knew that she would come back to them if she could not find food outside of the ark.

Japheth fetched the raven as he was ordered, but when he climbed up the ladder with the bird firmly clasped in his big hand, he discovered that his other family members had no intentions of being left out of this latest adventure.

Naamah had a worried look on her face. "Do you think you should do this?" she asked. "This bird has her young in the nest. It would be cruel to deprive them of their mother."

Noah nodded his head as he patted Naamah's shoulders. "She'll be all right," he said. "If she cannot find a place to rest where there is food, she'll come back to the ark."

"I hope you're right," said Naamah as she watched her husband unfasten the lashings that held one of the window coverings in place. A gust of frigid air hit them as the loosened cover blew inward. Noah gently took the raven in his hands, crooned to it several times, then lifted his arms and flung the black feathered bird out through

The Women of the Ark

the window. The women all gasped as they watched the raven flap its wings frantically, trying desperately to fight the heavy wind. Then, with a single, raucous cry, it took to the air and soon became nothing more than a dark spot in the sky. Over the next few hours the raven periodically came back to the ark, squawking noisily as it approached the open section of the window. Two or three times the bird alighted, but she seemed reluctant to reenter the ark. But finally, obviously exhausted from her fruitless search, the raven did land on the window sill.

Zolah reached out and grabbed the tired bird. "That's enough for today, little one," she said as she pressed her lips to the top of the bird's head. "Your chicks are hungry and want to snuggle under your wings."

A week passed before Noah decided to try again, but this time he sent out a dove. Once again the entire family climbed the ladder to the high window and watched with trepidation as Noah flung the white bird out into the open sky. The wind had died down, making it easier for the dove to glide down the side of the mountain.

The family sat beside the open portion of the window and waited anxiously for the dove to return. The morning passed, but there was no sign of the bird. They ate their noon meal in silence, then made their way back up to the opening. Still no sign of the dove. As the sun began to slide down the sky toward the western horizon, the men gave up and went below to do the many chores that had been left unattended. The women prepared the evening meal, but left most of it on the table uneaten for there was still some light in the sky and the dove may have returned. They opened only a small portion of the window for the air was growing extremely cold. Sitting there in the frigid air, they tried to lift each others spirits by telling amusing stories, but nothing could distract them from the worrisome fear that the dove had come to some harm out there in the cold, unforgiving world of the mountain.

As dark shadows began to gather around the base of the ark and the abyss below the mountain turned into an inky, black hole, Zolah declared that she was going back to their quarters to get some warm wraps. She was especially worried about Naamah, for the older woman could not tolerate the cold as easily as the others.

Naamah, Ophea and Rhema were determined to keep their watch by the window, praying that they would hear some small, promising sound that would mean that the dove had returned.

The wind was picking up again, blowing wisps of snow through the opening and leaving a blanket of drifted snow on the windowsill. A white, quarter-moon hung high in the sky, waiting for the darkness when its pale light would be strong enough to coat the surrounding mountain peaks with shimmering silver. And then, just as Naamah was wringing her hands in despair, fearful that the dove had been truly lost, there was the fluttering sound of wings over the roof of the ark. The women held their breaths and listened. Yes, there it was again, the fluttering of wings and then the soft cooing sound of the dove coming from somewhere above them.

"Zolah!" cried Naamah, "Come back! Quickly, child! Forget the wraps." She stopped to listen again as Zolah made her way quickly back up the ladder.

Zolah approached as quietly as she could, for she too was listening.

"Do you hear it?" asked Naamah. "Do you hear that soft cooing sound?"

Zolah clapped her hands together in triumph. "YES! Oh, Mother Naamah, she's come back to us!" She scrambled to the window and tried to wedge herself through the narrow opening. "She must be perched somewhere on the roof just above us," she called back to the others, "But I don't think she can find her way in. If we can't coax her to the window soon, it will be too dark to see her."

Ophea let out a small cry of despair. "Oh, dear, she'll freeze to death if she's out there all night. What can we do? Surely there must be something we can do to get her to come to the window!"

Dropping back down to the floor, Zolah reached over to pull one of the oil lamps off the hook on the wall where she had placed it just moments earlier. She had a special feeling for this gentle bird and hated the thought of having it lost now when it was so close to the safety of the ark. It was she who had tamed the dove by holding her hand in its cage to let it peck at the seeds that lay on her open palm. If the bird would come to anyone, Zolah felt certain it would come to her.

Pushing herself up on tip-toe, she leaned as far out of the window as she could and held out the lantern. "I think I see her," she said. She began to coo quietly as she coaxed the dove to come to her hand. "Quick, bring me some seeds. Surely she must be hungry," she said as she tried to squeeze herself further out the window.

Suddenly, Zolah let out a little shout of frustration as she let the lantern drop from her hand. They could hear it clatter down the side of the ark and hit the ice pack below with a low thud.

"She's almost to the top edge of the window, but I can't quite reach her!" wailed Zolah.

Naamah tugged at her daughter-in-law's skirts. "Zolah, get down!" she commanded. "You're leaning too far out and you'll fall. Wait and see if the dove comes in by herself."

Noah was just climbing up the ladder to see what all the commotion was about when he noticed Naamah frantically motioning for him to come help pull Zolah back in, for by now the younger woman was shaking so hard from the cold that she had all she could do to hold onto the edges of the window frame.

When her feet touched the deck, Zolah began to cry. "She's so close," she moaned. "But I—I can't quite reach her!"

Noah went to the window, thrust out his arm, and began to make the same, soft cooing noises that Zolah had used to try to coax the bird in. A smile creased his weathered, old cheeks. "Ah-ha!" he said with a twinkle in his eye, "This is a very smart dove, for she knows who her master is." Giving Naamah a conspiratorial wink, he pulled in his arm. There sat the dove, securely perched on the side of Noah's hand.

Trying to stifle a laugh, Naamah clasped her hands against her mouth then reached for the shivering bird. "What is this she's holding in her beak?" she asked. She gently pried the bit of twig out of the dove's mouth, then held it up in triumph for all to examine. The flickering lamplight was weak, but it was enough to see what the dove had brought back to them. There on the twig, small but distinctly green, were the tiny, newly sprouted leaves of an olive branch! [17]

The others wanted immediately to yank off the boards along the edges of the window to see if they could get out, but Noah was adamantly against the idea. "It's not yet safe enough," he proclaimed. "We'll wait one more week and send the dove out again."

The seven days passed with excruciating slowness. When the last day of the week came, everyone trudged back up the ladder. The air on the mountain was not quite as cold today. There was a bright sun glistening on the snow fields and a breeze that beckoned to them. Noah raised his hand and thrust the dove out the window. She mounted high into the sparkling, blue sky then made a steep dive, heading down with such purpose that they could not help but feel that she knew what she would find below.

The day passed and evening fell, but the dove did not return. When morning broke, a thick fog covered the top of the mountain so they could not even see the sky. The dove was gone, and though they waited throughout that day and the next, she did not come back to the ark.

"She's found a place of safety," declared Naamah with a knowing voice.

"Yes," answered Noah. "The earth is dry. Surely the time has come when God will release us."

"But how will we open the door?" asked Rhema. "It's such a massive thing. I doubt that the eight of us together could prize it open."

"Patience," answered Noah. "God will find a way."

Chapter Ten

All in God's Good Time

God's sunrise will break in upon us, shining on those in the darkness, those sitting in the shadow of death, then showing us the way one foot at a time, down the path of peace. Luke 1:79

Japheth cupped his hands and blew into them as he surveyed the circle of expectant faces. He could barely speak without taking deep gulps of air between every few words. "You—you'd better pray—pray hard—that—that there's a way down this mountain."

The exposed skin on Japheth's hands and face was already raw from the bitter wind that had battered him with gale-like force as he had tried to examine the outside terrain. "We're up high," he said. "I mean— really high! From what I can see between the cloud layers, we're lodged in tight. It looks like there are slabs of jagged rock or maybe ice pressing hard against the entire lower portion of the ark." He hesitated and blew into his hands again as he tried to think of a gentle way to break the news. "I'm sorry, but I don't see any way out of here."

"WHAT?" shouted Ham as he slammed his fist against a wooden beam. "You have to be joking! By all that's holy, why would God make us go through all of this only to abandon us on top of a pile of rocks and ice?"

Ophea reached out and placed a restraining hand on Ham's shoulder. "The door, Japheth—what of the door? Please, can't we at least try to open the door?"

Japheth shook his head in despair. "I—I don't know, Ophea. It's hard to tell."

"WHAT DO YOU MEAN YOU DON'T KNOW?" shouted Ham. "The door is just below the place where you were standing. Surely it must have been in plain sight. Couldn't you have at least taken the time to check out the door?" He turned to look at the others then he spun around again towards Japheth. "All right, if you can't manage it, then perhaps someone else needs to go up there and take a look."

"EXACTLY!" shouted Japheth. "AND I THINK IT SHOULD BE YOU!" He pushed himself upright, rubbed his hands briskly on his pant legs, and walked over to the wall under the opening. Leaning over and cupping his clasped hands, he turned to face Ham. "All right, come on over here and let me give you a hand up. As long as you think it's so simple why don't you just climb outside and take a really good look! Let's see how you like the taste of ice between your teeth!"

Ham glared at his brother and started walking toward him, but instead of placing his foot in Japheth's hands, he suddenly grasped a fistful of his brother's cloak and pushed him hard against the wall. "I've had about enough of you," he said, spitting out the words. "Since when do you give the orders around here? If I needed your help, I'd ask. Now get out of my way so I can go out there and find out exactly what the problem is."

With a cry of fear, Rhema ran forward and grasped Ham's shoulder. "Please, Ham, don't try it. You heard what Japheth said; there's nothing but slabs of ice and rocks out there. If you should fall . . . ."

"OUT OF MY WAY, WOMAN!" Ham roughly pushed Rhema away. "I've had enough of the lot of you cowards. God says this and God says that. I say it's about time we took our fate into our own hands!"

Naamah let out a gasp as she reached down to comfort Rhema who had fallen to the floor and was sobbing as though her heart was broken. What blasphemy was this? Could Ham have so easily forgotten how God had led them safely through so many trials? How could he have forgotten the terrors of the deluge and the salvation that God had given them?

The Women of the Ark

Finally, Noah stepped forward, reached out to Ham and gently turned him around. "There is no need for this, my son. The Lord knows how much we wish to be out of the ark. He understands the pressures we are all under. We've been cooped up here together, but this is not the time to lose patience, Ham. The Lord brought us all this long way. He has a plan to release us onto an earth made clean and new, free from sin and hatred. But it must be in His time and according to His will, my son."

Noah voiced what they were all feeling, for it had been so long since they had put their feet on solid ground. How they longed to stand under a wide, blue sky and feel the soft touch of a gentle breeze caress their cheeks. Whenever there was a break in the clouds and blowing ice, the breathtaking landscape of jagged, snow-covered mountain peaks was an awesome sight. The shear majesty of this rugged landscape was something they had never seen before. Also, the harsh air at this altitude was thin and bitterly cold, making breathing difficult and increasing the amount of energy required for even the simplest of physical tasks. Worst of all were the constant winds that howled and moaned around the ark like beasts of prey.

Yes, Noah understood their frustration. He, too, wondered how they would ever make their way down such treacherous slopes. He, too, longed to once again stand knee-deep in a meadow filled with sweet-smelling grasses and wild flowers, to hear the trilling of song birds in the trees, and to watch a flock of sheep grazing upon a gently sloping hill. Night after night he dreamed of sinking to his knees on the sun-warmed earth as he lifted his voice in praise to the God that he loved with all of his heart and soul.

Patience, they must have patience, with God and with each other. How many times had Noah urged his family to take one day at a time and await the good will of the Lord. Surely even Ham, this son of his who was so quick to anger, knew that their very survival would be an incomprehensible miracle and that absolutely nothing was impossible with God. Now, lifting his arms in supplication, Noah bent his head in prayer and asked that the Lord would again intervene and deliver them from the top of the mountain peak.

Momentarily shamed by their father's deep faith and their own angry outbursts, Ham and Japheth hung their heads and waited for

Noah to finish his prayer, but sadly, their remorse was short-lived. Riled by the thought that Ham had accused him of being a coward, Japheth went back to the window and began ripping off several of the upper boards with his bare hands. When he was satisfied that the opening was large enough, he took a deep breath, hoisted himself up through the enlarged opening, and tried to wriggle out. With nothing to grasp onto but the icy, wooden planks, his perch was precarious at the very least.

Naamah let out a gasp of fear. "OH, JAPTHETH, PLEASE, COME BACK!" she shouted. "YOU'RE GOING TO FALL!"

Japtheth must have heard her, for he managed to wedge his left arm back in, and he waved in the general direction of the waiting family.

"WHAT CAN YOU SEE NOW?" shouted Shem. "HOW BAD IS THE DAMAGE?"

Japheth's response was blown away by the wind. He kicked hard with his legs, and he managed to squeeze his body further out of the broken window frame.

Again, Naamah let out a frightened cry. Rhema wrapped her arms around her mother-in-law's shoulders. "He'll be all right, Mother," she whispered, though she herself was greatly concerned for her husband's safety.

"CAN YOU SEE THE DOOR YET?" shouted Ham. "DO THE ROCKS BLOCK IT? MAYBE WE CAN PRY IT OPEN!"

Japheth tried to answer, but once again his words were swept away as soon as he spoke them. Squirming back in through the broken window frame, he dropped to the floor and gasped for breath. His cheeks were beginning to blister from the cutting wind, and a thin line of ice covered his lashes and eyebrows. Sitting with his arms crossed in front of his chest, fists clenched, Japheth could only gasp for breath and shake his head.

"Well," said Ham, belligerent as ever. "Can we get out of this thing or not?"

Naamah gave Ham a stern look while pulling off her shawl and wrapping it around Japheth's trembling shoulders. "Please, Ham, can't you give him a moment?" she said. "Surely you can see that he's blue with the cold!"

It was Zolah who finally put words to their greatest concern. "Oh!" she wailed as she pressed her hands to her face. "How will we get the animals out? And the birds, our poor birds, and the little mice—and—and, oh, dear, Mother Naamah, what shall we ever do?"

"God will provide," said Noah, giving Naamah no chance to reply. This time his voice was stern with reproach. "After all that we've been through, have you no faith, my children?" Shaking his head in despair, he turned and walked to the railing. He peered down into the dark recesses of the ark. How much more of this could his family withstand, he wondered? Was he to lose them now when they were so close to the end of their great odyssey?

Naamah, still shaken by Japheth's daring actions and Ham's volatile temper, decided that it was time to get her daughter-in-laws to a safer location. On the pretext that she needed their help in the kitchen, she directed the three young women to follow her down the ladder. Truth be told, Naamah did not particularly like having other women working in her kitchen, even if they were her own kin. She felt that whatever was about to happen on this upper deck would be best left for her husband to deal with.

Ham didn't wait until the women were out of earshot, for his anger at his brother still simmered just below the surface. "YOU!" he shouted, spinning around to face Japheth. "ALWAYS THE BIG HERO, AREN'T YOU! TRYING TO MAKE ME LOOK LIKE AN INCOMPETENT SIMPLETON!" Now he had his fists raised, and Japheth, never one to turn from a challenge, did likewise.

"JAPHETH! HAM! ENOUGH OF THIS!" Noah was a man of peace, but he could be stern when it was needed, especially with his sons. "If you cannot be men enough to keep these heated discussions between yourselves, then you'd best go down into the hold and fight this out properly. I do not, under any circumstance, want you arguing like this in front of the women, especially now!"

"Ha! And why **not** now?" snapped Ham. Stepping forward, he raised his arm and pressed his hand against the post that his father was leaning on so he could glare down at him. Ham's insubordination toward his father had been growing steadily in the past few weeks, and now his undisguised disdain was painfully obvious.[18]

"So tell me, Father," he asked, "What's the difference? Why should the women be any more frightened now than they were before?"

Cutting his eyes angrily toward Japheth and then Shem, Ham let out a derisive laugh. "Perhaps these two must do their wives' bidding, but no mere woman can keep me under her thumb."

Ham thrust out his hands in disgust, then turned on his heel and began to stalk away. If he had left it at that, perhaps his angry words would have been forgotten, but Ham was not one to let his temper cool easily. Suddenly he spun back around and took one more jab at his astonished father. His voice was low, but not so low that his brothers missed his last cutting remark. "A fine example you are, Old Man. Between you, your god and our mother, it's a wonder you can even think for yourself anymore!"

Satisfied that he had finally put his father in his place, Ham squared his shoulders, turned and began to walk away. But before he had gone more than a few paces, a peal of thunder tore across the heavens. The entire ark let out a loud groan and then a heart-stopping crash came from somewhere far below. There was another thunderous boom followed by a sickening scrapping sound as the great vessel shifted and moved.

Shem let out a shout as he reached for a nearby railing. "WE'RE SLIDING!" he shouted. "THE ARK IS SLIDING DOWN THE MOUNTAIN!"

On the decks and floors below, panic reigned. The women let out cries of terror as the ark lurched first to one side and then the other. A cacophony of howls, yelps and caterwauling screams erupted from the many cages and pens of the confined animals and birds. The horrific noises of splintering wood were followed by the percussive sounds of pottery and earthen vessels crashing to the floor. The frightening noises reverberated throughout the ark. From deep below came a rapid salvo of explosive noise as massive wooden beams cracked and tore loose. The ark keeled over to a forty-five degree angle and stopped, held in place by, only God in heaven knew what!

Somehow, Shem managed to right himself. He clawed his way to the top of the ladder, turned once to be certain that his father was safe, then disappeared over the side. Afraid that the women had

The Women of the Ark

been injured, he knew he must get to them as quickly as possible. No sooner had he gone below, than the ark shifted again. Unable to maintain his grasp on the rail, Noah teetered over the gaping hole where a portion of the deck had suddenly given way. Reacting out of sheer instinct, Japheth managed to grab his father's arm and pull him backward. They both landed with a sickening thud on the hard floor of the deck.

Ham, in the meantime, struggled to remain upright. He grasped at a swinging rope and tried to hold on, but the shifting of the ark had broken the restraining straps that held secure one of Naamah's large planting boxes. With a cry of dismay, Ham let go of the rope and leaped into the air as the heavy box came hurtling across the tilting deck, heading straight for him. He jumped clear of the box, but when he landed, his feet gave way beneath him, causing him to plunge forward onto his hands and knees. Tears of pain sprang to his eyes, but he could not utter a word, for he was too busy gasping for air.

The moments of terror passed as suddenly as they had come. With another great groan, the ark righted itself and settled back into place. Surely God had spoken, but what had He said?

Ham dragged himself to his feet and limped painfully toward the window where he remained for some time starring out into the swirling haze of wind-driven snow. His shoulders slumped forward, and he shook all over, but still he made no effort to turn around and look at his father.

Noah allowed Japheth to help him to his feet. He hurt everywhere, but his greatest pain was for his beloved, youngest son. Tears of regret coursed down his cheeks. He stretched out his hands toward Ham as though to draw him in, but he could find no words to say that would undo what had just happened. What *could* he say to a son who had so obviously rejected him?

Trying to soothe over the uncomfortable situation, Jahpeth rested his hand on Noah's shoulder. "Father," he said, "Just leave him be." He took in a deep breath, then reached for Noah's trembling arm. "Come," he said as gently as he could. "We must go down and see if the women are unharmed."

Noah hesitated for just a moment. A look of deep longing came upon his face as he stared at Ham's slumped shoulders.

"Please, Father," whispered Japheth. "Ham needs some time to himself. Here, let me help you down the ladder. Watch your step, there may be some rungs that have pulled loose."

The floors of the ark were slippery with spilled water mixed with bits of hay and animal waste. Thankfully, no fires had started. Many of the oil lamps had gone out leaving the passageways dark with shadows. Noah and Japheth picked their way through the rubble, groping for the rails of the animal pens and the safety ropes that had been strung along the walls.

When they reached their living quarters, they were stunned by the mass of broken pots and spilled provisions that covered the now tilted shelves and most of the floor. The large table where they ate their meals had been partially ripped loose. It sat at a lopsided angle; the bowls and plates that had been laid out upon it now lay in jagged pieces on the floor. The chaos of the room was heightened by the dancing flames that leaped from the fire pit sending a shower of red sparks toward the ceiling. Thankfully, none of the burning logs had fallen out of the pit, but there appeared to be a large crack in the mud and stone chimney that could, if left unattended, be extremely dangerous.

Poor Noah and Japheth would have found it a most discouraging sight, if it weren't for the women. There they were, frightened, disheveled, unsteady on their feet, yet busily trying to clean up the worst of the mess. Noah reached out to Naamah and pulled her into his arms. "My poor, dear wife," he said tenderly as he kissed her forehead. "What I have put you through!"

"Husband," answered Naamah, "You have put me through nothing that I would not go through all over again, for all of these trials have been ordained by God and must be borne. But He has seen us through far worse than this, Husband. Surely this will end soon. Surely He will not let this voyage end in tragedy. What good would we be to Him dead and buried under the broken timbers of this ark?"

Worry lines were furrowed across Noah's forehead. "Beloved wife," he whispered, "I have prayed long and hard for God's deliverance, and surely He has heard my pleas for help. But if He should choose to bury us upon the top of this mountain, I will die in peace knowing that you are at my side." He brushed the loose strands of hair away from Naamah's face and rubbed a smudge of soot from her forehead. He could feel the quivering of her body. The truth of it was that his own legs were so shaky that it was all he could do to remain standing. "Come," he said. "Come over here and rest yourself. We are in God's hands." Guiding Naamah to the one bench that remained upright, he sat down and pulled her onto his lap.

Naamah's head drooped upon her husband's shoulder, as his calloused, old hands protectively covered hers. They sat there quietly for several moments, neither one of them able to speak, but gaining solace from the deep love that united them.

Naamah felt more exhausted than she'd ever felt before. Finally, with her head still resting on Noah's bony shoulder and her hands lying limp in his, she let out a long sigh, closed her eyes, and realized that she was even too spent to cry.

"Husband," she said, her voice barely audible, "I try so hard to hold onto my faith, but—but, there are times when I have such terrible doubts. How much more of this must we endure?"

For once, Noah had no answer. He simply sat there stroking her hands and rubbing his soft beard against her hair. He started humming a wordless tune, giving the kind of comfort that a father might give to a frightened child. Slowly, the shadows of the evening began to cover them, smoothing the lines from their faces and resting gently upon their hunched shoulders.

Japheth went to the chimney to temporarily shore it up. He rearranged the logs in the fire pit, examined the ceiling to be certain that the sparks had gone out, and did a quick check of the great casks that held their precious drinking water. When he was certain that everything was secure, he pulled a soft fleece from one of the cupboards and draped it gently around the huddled forms of his parents. They sat there with their eyes closed, not seeming to notice that anyone else was in the room.

Sympathetic to their deep exhaustion and the moments of weakness that they had endured, Japheth called quietly to the younger women, beckoning them to come with him out of the room. When they were standing together in the wide corridor that led to the pens of the smaller animals, Japheth told them what had occurred between Ham and his father.

Zolah pressed her hands to her face and began to cry while Rhema pounded one fisted hand into the open palm of the other. But poor Ophea could only gape at Japheth as she shook her head with helpless concern. More and more she was coming to fear her husband's increasing caustic behavior. His actions did not bode well for their future together. She could not even imagine what it would be like living with him once they were off the ark and on their own.

Practical as ever, Rhema pulled her two sisters-in-law together and started giving them a crisp set of orders. "Zolah," she said, "you must go quickly and check the cages of the smaller animals. Some of the grates and bars may have come loose." She reached out and grasped Ophea's arm. "Look here, my dear sister, there'll be time enough later to think of how you will handle your husband, but for now, there is much work to be done. And as long as he's up there brooding, there's little you can do to change his thinking. I'd suggest that you leave that to God." She tried to keep her voice level and firm. In reality, Rhema felt a deep concern for this woman whom she had come to know so well. Despite all of the times that she had gotten angry and frustrated over Ophea's inability to show her true emotions, Rhema was now determined that she would do whatever she could to protect her sister-in-law from the coming troubles that seemed inevitable. For now, however, it surely would be best to get Ophea's mind off of her worries, and what better way to do it than to set her to work.

Zolah, of course, needed no further encouragement. Worried sick about the smaller creatures confined on the ark, she grabbed up an oil lamp and hurried toward the row of cages where they were housed. She was especially concerned about those who were with young, for their very presence was surely sign enough that it was time to leave the ark. With the food supply quickly disappearing, God *had* to find a way to get them all safely down the face of this mountain!

Chapter Eleven

I Do Set My Bow in the Clouds

*This is the sign of the covenant I am making
between me and you and everything living around you and
everyone living after you. I am putting my rainbow in the clouds,
a sign of the covenant between me and the Earth. From now on,
when I form a cloud over the Earth and the rainbow appears in the
cloud, I'll remember my covenant between me and you and every
living thing, that never again will flood waters destroy all life.
When the rainbow appears in the cloud, I'll see it and remember
the eternal covenant between God and everything living,
every last living creature on Earth. Genesis 9:12-16*

Early the next morning the members of Noah's family were standing on the upper deck peering anxiously out of the enlarged opening. They had loosened more of the boards and pulled them away so they now had a clear view. Even Ham was there, and for once, he had lost some of his churlishness and actually seemed a bit embarrassed by the harsh behavior he had exhibited the night before.

Despite the chilly air, an expectancy of something mysterious and wonderful seemed to flood through the open window. All eyes eagerly scanned the distant horizon with a look of great yearning. Noah and his entire family prayed earnestly for a sign of hope. "Just one sign, Lord," they prayed. "Just one small sign to let us know that You have not deserted us."

As they were watching, the cloud cover on the eastern horizon began to change. Its color turned from an icy gray to a deep purple and then to a lavender-blue. The thick haze that hung high in the heavens began to disperse, and one by one the brightest stars of the eastern sky began to flicker and then blaze into view.

The family was spell-bound as they watched the drama of pending dawn, for it had been days since they had seen the sun. Ever since the dove had left them, a heavy haze had covered the top of the mountain and obliterated the sky. They longed for a clear view of the eastern horizon, for surely they would be able to see dry land somewhere out there in the distance.

Slowly, the sky lightened and one by one the stars flickered and faded from view. Only the bright glow of the morning star held its own against the coming of day, but soon it too was swallowed up by the growing light.

And then, suddenly, the real drama began! The curtains of night slid away as bright beams of light pierced the cloud-cover that had hung so tenaciously around the peaks of the surrounding mountains. The air began to soften with just the faintest touch of warmth. And with a burst of brilliant energy, the massive orb of the sun slid over the horizon.

In unison, the members of Noah's family let out a great shout of joy. They lifted their faces to the rays of sunlight, bathing their skin with its warmth. Wide beams of light bounced off the sheets of ice that encased the top of the mountain that grasped the ark so firmly. The outer planking of the great vessel began to glisten like burnished gold as the sky above turned from white to azure blue. A familiar song of praise went up from the lips of those standing at the open window.

How beautiful the earth!
How wondrous the sky!
Now praise Him, praise Him,
Lift your voices on high.

For it is He who is Lord
Over earth, sea and sky.

As they sang, the women wrapped their arms about each other, embracing the close companionship they shared, for they had come through violent storms and the raging flood—together. They had proved themselves strong and filled with courage—together. They had overcome obstacles that few women had ever faced. Theirs was a bond born of great travail. And because of it, they would never again be the fearful women who had first entered the ark.

Zolah reached out and threw her arms around Naamah. Giving her daughter-in-law a warm smile, Naamah turned and reached for the sunlight. As in the days before the flood, when she would greet each morning by standing at her doorstep to watch the rising of the sun, so now she greeted this glorious morning, where surely, there was the smell of freedom.

Noah pulled his family close for their morning prayers. It was a long, established habit that had seen them through some of their darkest hours. And now, with the glorious sunlight streaming through the window, it seemed especially appropriate.

Just as they were starting to turn away, a distant, high-pitched sound caught the attention of those still near the window. It seemed to be coming from an unusually bright spot of sky on the eastern horizon.

"What is it?" asked Ophea. She pressed herself against the window ledge and lifted her hand above her eyes to shield them, for the sunlight glanced off the ice floes with such intensity that it was hard to see much beyond their own mountain peak.

"Perhaps it's your sign," said Ham, resuming the mocking voice that had, of late, become his trademark. "Although how the rising of the sun can be a sign is quite beyond me," he added.

"No," answered Ophea. "Didn't you hear it? It's not the sunshine. Listen, it's a shrill sound, and it's getting louder!"

And then, they all could hear it. It grew so intense that it battered against their eardrums with such force that they had to clap their hands over the sides of their heads.

"LOOK!" shouted Rhema as she ran back toward the window and pointed toward the horizon. "LOOK AT THAT BRILLIANT BALL OF LIGHT! WHY, IT'S COMING RIGHT AT US—IT'S GETTING - - -."

She was unable to finish the sentence, for the very air around them was splintered as the great ball of light screeched across the sky and slammed into the side of the ark with such force that the massive vessel was almost dislodged from the great boulders that held it in place. First they heard a horrendous wrenching noise, and then an explosive **CLAP**!

"THE DOOR!" shouted Shem as he raced across the deck and took the ladder two rungs at a time. "LOOK! LOOK! THE DOOR'S BEEN OPENED!"

As the family rushed down to the lower deck, they began to shout with joy as they discovered brilliant shafts of sunlight streaming through the wide opening, flooding the darkest recesses of the ark. They stood at the gaping hole where once the massive door had stood and lifted their arms in sheer wonder. Then, spontaneously, the women grabbed each other and began dancing about, laughing and shouting, as they weaved first one way and then the other.

A low rumbling noise stopped them in their tracks. "What is it?" asked Naamah, her joy suddenly turned to fear, for the noise was growing ever more ominous. "Now what?"

Just then the entire top of the mountain seemed to shake and vibrate as the rumbling grew to an ear-splitting roar. Great clouds of ice and snow spewed up into the heavens, entirely obliterating the sunlight and cutting off their view of everything outside the ark. This roaring and shaking of the mountain seemed to last for a very long time. But then, the noise began to abate, and the clouds of snow slowly settled into place.

Holding onto each other for dear life, the family edged cautiously toward the vast space of the open doorway. Their jaws hung down, and their eyes popped wide in amazement. Before them lay a wide, smooth pathway that led all the way down to the valley below!

"Wha—what's happened?" Shem, blurted out but there was no need for anyone to answer his question, for it was all quite obvious. The explosive opening of the door had started a massive avalanche of such proportions that the entire ragged face of the mountain had been torn away. In its place, miracle of miracles, there was the very means of escape that, just moments earlier, they had thought quite impossible. God had created their pathway to safety! Surely His voice was in that powerful beam of light that had opened the door of the ark.

"Leave the ship," it said to Noah, "you and your wife and your sons and your son's wives. And take all the animals with you, the whole menagerie of birds and mammals and crawling creatures, all that brimming prodigality of life, so they can reproduce and flourish on the Earth."

The procession that came down the mountain on that glorious day was something to behold! The family of Noah gathered up the cages and pens of all of the smaller creatures—the mice and the rabbits; the birds, moths and butterflies; the tiniest moles, crickets and beetles. They placed the slithering snakes and soft-skinned lizards in earthen vessels; they made cages of reeds for the newly-hatched chicks, and they made pens of sticks for the newborn monkeys, squirrels and ferrets. Every small, tender creature that had been housed in the ark was carefully accounted for. Then, placing the pens and vessels onto the larger animals, they strapped them securely with the hemp ropes that had been used to fasten together the partitions in the ark. And so the procession began.

What a sight! Surely, thought Naamah with delight, God in His heaven and the His entire host of angels must be chuckling and laughing out loud at the sight of this great spectacle!

As the procession reached the first plateau, already a verdant green with new shoots of grass, an even more marvelous thing happened. Noah stopped the entourage, for he would go no further without erecting an altar to the God who had saved them. Their worship service was suddenly alight with the most glorious colors they had ever seen. Looking up into the sky to discover the source of this marvelous light, tears of wonder and delight sprang to their eyes. For there, stretched across the breadth of the heavens was an arch of scintillating colors such as they had never seen before in all of the years that had gone before the flood: **A Bow! A great and glorious Bow!**

The marveling spectators could hardly fathom what this amazing phenomenon could be, but God did not leave them wondering for long. Like the rumbling of thunder that breaks through gathering storm clouds, His voice came down to them, echoing and reverberating from mountain peak to mountain peak.

"This is the sign of the covenant I am making between me and you and everything living around you and everyone living after you. I am putting my rainbow in the clouds, a sign of the covenant between me and the Earth. From now on, when I form a cloud over the Earth and the rainbow appears in the cloud, I'll remember my covenant between me and you and everything living, that never again will floodwaters destroy all life. When the rainbow appears in the cloud, I'll see it and remember the eternal covenant between God and every living thing, every last living creature on Earth."[19]

When the long line of animals finally reached the bright meadow that spread out for mile after mile about the foot of the mountains, the family began to open the cages and pens that they had strapped onto the backs of the larger mammals. The birds took to the sky en masse, filling it with their joyous songs at having been released from their long captivity. The moths and butterflies followed them. Within moments they were fluttering about in vibrant clouds of color over the myriads of wildflowers that covered the meadowland. Both small and large animals cavorted through the sweet grasses and rolled about amongst the tender shoots of new plant life. They splashed into the brook that babbled and sang as it meandered through the meadow. They dived into the crystal-clear lake that lay in a great depression left by the flood waters.

And just as spontaneous as the animals, the family of Noah began to dance and run through the fields, reaching out to throw their arms around tender saplings that some day soon would turn into shaded woodlands and vast forests. They buried their faces in sweet-smelling flowers and lifted their heads to take great gulps of the soft, fresh air that blew around them. Their shouts of joy and laughter carried up through the Earth's bright firmament, and their prayers of thanksgiving were lifted up on wings of song all the way to the very gates of Heaven!

Standing in the warm sunlight with a soft wind blowing and the delightful smell of wild flowers wafting around them, Naamah drew her daughters-in-law close to her. She looked into the eyes of each one in turn, these women who had endured so much and who had grown so mightily in moral strength and beauty of character: Rhema, the eldest of the three, a woman of wit, physical strength and unquestionable courage. Ophea, the one whose husband had caused them such worry and heartache, yet through it all, she had preserved her faith and grown in wisdom and self-confidence. Zola, the youngest of the three who had known such personal torment, yet had overcome the terrors of her past now standing firm and tall in the knowledge that she was indeed worthy of being loved and cherished.

"Gather close, my daughters," said Naamah, "for there is a matter of great importance that I must share with you. Each of us, in our own way, has turned this voyage of faith into an experience that has made us what we now are. And we are *not* the same women who entered the ark. Oh, no! Now, my daughters, we are indeed the keepers of the family of man. But there is more—much more, for you see, we must also be the keepers of the faith that brought us through to this time of celebration. These are responsibilities that carry both heavy burdens and great honors. For you see, dear ones, it is you—each one of you—who must pass the story of what we have experienced to your children and your children's children. Long after you've left this world, even unto the time that the earth has waxed old and the coming of The Promised One has been fulfilled, you, my daughters, will be remembered."

Naamah smiled gently as she placed her hands in blessing first on one bowed head and then the other. "Oh, yes, it is true that your names may well be lost to memory, but the fact that you kept the faith and honored the covenant will live on through all of the years of earth's history and even into eternity. Go then, my dear ones. Go and let the world know that you are not only women of great moral strength and courage, but also keepers of the faith!"

End Notes

All verses quoted in the following end notes are from the New International Version (NIV) Bible.

1 Preface, page vi: Noah's wife is not named in Scripture, however, the name I have chosen for the wife of Noah is Naamah. This same name may be found in the 4th chapter of Genesis, which gives the generations of Cain. Cain begot Enoch, Enoch begot Irad, Irad begot Mehujael, Mehujael begot Methushael, Methushael begot Lamech. Verse 19 states that Lamech had two wives: Adah and Zilah. Verse 22 reads: "Zilah also had a son Tubal-Cain, who forged all kinds of tools out of bronze and iron. Tubal-Cain's sister was **Naamah**."

[2] Chapter One, page 2: Various commentaries and Bible dictionaries state that the Hebrew word for "ark" is of Egyptian origin. The Egyptian "arks" were large seaworthy vessels capable of carrying the massive stones and obelisks from their places of origin down the Nile to the locations where the pyramids were being constructed. The ark also is a representation of Christ who is, for those who accept Him, the refuge from God's judgment for sin.

[3] Chapter One, page 5: While Shem is mentioned first in Genesis 5:32, most commentators refer to Genesis 9:22-24, which clearly identifies Ham as the youngest son, and Genesis 10:21, that speaks of Japtheth as being the eldest. It was, however, from Shem's lineage that the chosen people of God came, and it was also through his line that the promised Messiah was to come. Thus, Genesis 5:32 is seen as a testament to the importance of Shem as the forefather of the coming Deliverer.

[4] Chapter Two, page 9: God's directions for the building of the ark were as complete and perfect as His original creation of the Earth and its inhabitants. The dimensions listed in Genesis 6:15 is given in cubits as follows: length – 300 cubits, width – 50 cubits, and height (depth) – 30 cubits. To determine the actual size of the ark in feet, compute 1 cubit as 18 inches. Thus, the ark was 450 feet

The Women of the Ark

long, the width of its beam was 75 feet, and its depth was 45 feet. This is comparable to the size of a modern day ocean liner!

[5] Chapter Two, page 13: Some might question whether Noah and his sons had the capabilities and tools necessary to hew massive trees, and then saw, plane and shape them into the planks, stanchions and furnishings described in this narrative. Referring once again to Genesis 4:22 we read that Tubal-Cain, the son of Lamech, "forged all kinds of tools out of bronze and iron." Due to the total destruction that took place during the deluge, we have no known archeological evidence that the civilization that existed prior to the flood was highly advanced in the arts and sciences. However, the Bible clearly tells us that the antediluvians were skilled craftsman who had metal tools strong enough to effectively carry out the task of building such a large vessel. Also, Adam and Eve were created by the hand of God as physically and mentally perfect humans with superior intelligence and physical strength. Noah was just ten generations away from Adam and Eve, thus, the human gene pool, although already under the pernicious influences of sin, was surely not as blighted as it is today. Noah and his sons most certainly must have had superior intelligence, strength and creative capabilities. This physical and mental superiotity would also explain the longevity of life enjoyed by the antediluvians.

[6] Chapter Two, page 23: In Genesis 9:20 we read: "Noah, a man of the soil, proceeded to plant a vineyard." While this verse tells of Noah's activities after the flood, it is also likely that he was involved in similar agricultural pursuits before the flood. It is interesting to note that archeological evidence and modern scientific studies have confirmed that viticulture most likely began close to Mount Ararat in the Asian portion of Turkey known as Anatolia. An ancient Hittite relief found in this area depicts King Tubal, a descendent of Japheth (Genesis 10:2), praying to the god of fertility who is holding stalks of wheat and a large bunch of grapes in his hands.

[7] Chapter Three, page 30: Despite the abhorrent behavior and extreme wickedness of mankind before the flood, God had found a man whom He could entrust with the future of the Earth. Genesis 6:8-9 reads: "But Noah found favor in the eyes of the Lord . . . Noah was a righteous man, blameless among the people of his time, and he walked with God." Herein is one of the finest tributes that a man can have in his relationship to his Heavenly Father. The word "blameless" does not mean that Noah was sinless. It does, however, tell us that he was a man of great religious strength and moral integrity. The fact that Noah could remain pious in the midst of such violence and wickedness is a testament to his fearless character. Indeed, that he had the fortitude to continue to plead with the antediluvians to repent through all the years that it took to build the ark speaks volumes about his relationship with his Creator. In turn, God's great love for His creation and His mercy toward mankind is seen in this miraculous act of saving Noah and his family from destruction.

The Women of the Ark

[8] Chapter Three, page 31: Though gopher wood is not known today, it is possible that it was timber from a coniferous tree such as cypress or cedar. Both of these woods are resinous and, thus, would be ideal for a sea-going vessel.

[9] Chapter Three, page 31: While we cannot be certain as to the exact appearance of the window in the ark, it is highly unlikely that it was the small aperture portrayed in the many fanciful renditions of this vessel. In the directions given by God for the construction of the ark, the King James Version of Genesis 6:16 reads: "A window shalt thou make to the ark, and in a cubit shalt thou finish it above." This description leaves room for a great deal of confusion. A better translation of this same text is found in the New International Version, which reads: "Make a roof for it and finish the ark to within eighteen inches of the top." Thus, we can visualize a long window going around the entire perimeter of the ark just under the edge of its roof. Such an opening would be necessary for illumination and the flow of fresh air. In this narrative, I have envisioned strong leather shades that could be rolled up for light and air and lashed tightly down during the heavy rain storms. While this is my interpretation, it is reasonable to assume that God would have made proper provision for the health, comfort and well-being of the people and animals confined in the ark.

[10] Chapter Three, page 36: The "Bride-Price" was the money paid to the parents of a young woman who had been seduced by a man before she was betrothed. See Exodus 22:16-17.

[11] Chapter Three, page 42: One of the most startling revelations of the story of Noah is the entrance of representative creatures of the Earth into the ark. That this amazing event took place in such an orderly fashion is overwhelming evidence that God was directing them. It is appalling to think that the people who observed this miraculous event were not shaken to their very core. What a contrast! If dumb beast could instantaneously respond to their Creator's call while intelligent human beings refused to listen to His warnings for more than one-hundred years, it is no wonder that God had no choice but to destroy mankind!

[12] Chapter Four, page 43: Genesis 7:2-3 reads: "Take with you seven of every kind of clean animal, a male and its mate, and two of every kind of unclean animal, a male and its mate, and also seven of every kind of bird, male and female, to keep their various kinds alive throughout the earth." Though the laws recorded by Moses in Leviticus 11 delineating clean from unclean animals were, to our knowledge, not written prior to the flood, it is obvious that these restriction were known by Noah. God instructed him to bring into the ark a larger number of clean animals and fowl, for once the flood was over they would be needed for food and sacrificial offerings.

[13] Chapter Five, page 64: Genesis 7:16 clearly states: "Then the LORD shut him in." This was not a simple closing of the door by Noah and his sons; it was a spectacular and miraculous act carried out by the hand of God. This was the divine pronouncement that the door of mercy was finally and irrevocably closed!

The Women of the Ark

[14] Chapter Five, page 67: This was no mere local event, but a catastrophic flood of worldwide dimensions. The story of this great flood is found in the legends of almost every race on Earth. The most notable of these flood "legends" was recorded by the ancient Babylonians who lived in the area around Mount Ararat where, after the flood, the human race once again began to proliferate.

[15] Chapter Six, page 78: Genesis 9:3 reads: "Everything that lives and moves will be food for you." The antediluvians were flesh eaters, but it wasn't until after the flood that God gave his permission for mankind to eat the meat of animals. Nevertheless, there were still certain restrictions. God said: "But you must not eat meat that has its lifeblood still in it." Genesis 9:4. (see also endnote 11)

[16] Chapter Eight, page 99: Lal is a type of honey derived from the sap of the date palm. The ancient Sumerians used it as their primary sweetener for baking and cooking.

[17] Chapter Nine, page 126: Genesis 8:11 reads: When the dove returned to him in the evening, there in its beak was a freshly plucked olive leaf." The fact that the leaf was fresh and green indicates that this was not simply from a branch that had somehow survived the flood and was floating about on the surface of the water. Fresh vegetation was again growing upon the drying surface of the Earth!

[18] Chapter Ten, page 134: Unfortunately, Ham, Noah's youngest son, did not follow his father's example of upright behavior. In Genesis 9:20-27 we find the sad story of Noah's sin of drunkenness, but sadder still is Ham's act of disrespect for his father, an indication of his lascivious character. This act was a precursor to the wickedness that would once more come upon mankind through the descendents of Ham. Genesis 9:22 reads: "Ham the father of Canaan, saw his father's nakedness and told his two brothers outside." Japheth and Shem, though stunned by their father's shameful condition, were even more appalled by their younger brother's reactions. When Noah awoke and realized what had taken place, he pronounced a curse on the descendents of Ham that proved terribly prophetic. The Canaanites, as Ham's descendents came to be called, would soon display a national propensity toward corrupt and wicked behavior.

[19] Chapter Eleven, page 146: This beautiful passage is found in Genesis 9:12-16.

The first appearance of the rainbow is further evidence that there was no rain prior to the flood. It was to be a sign and covenant between God and man, a symbol of God's great mercy and love for mankind. There are three other references to the rainbow found in the Bible. The first two describe the rainbow as encircling the heavenly throne of God:

"Like the appearance of a rainbow in the clouds on a rainy day, so was the radiance around him. This was the appearance of the likeness of the glory of the LORD. When I saw it, I fell facedown, and I heard the voice of one speaking." Ezekiel 1:28

"And the one who sat there had the appearance of jasper and carnelian. A rainbow, resembling an emerald, encircled the throne." Revelation 4:3

The third reference is a description of Christ at the final judgment of mankind: "Then I saw another mighty angel coming down from heaven. He was robed in a cloud, with a rainbow above his head; his face was like the sun, and his legs were like fiery pillars.

Revelation 10:1

Thus we read in Luke 17:26-27: "Just as it was in the days of Noah, so also will it be in the days of the Son of Man. People were eating, drinking, marrying and being given in marriage up to the day Noah entered the ark. Then the flood came and destroyed them all."

Resources & References

Dooley. Tom, 2005, *The True Story of Noah's Ark,* Master Books, Inc., Green Forest, AR

Freeman, James, 1996, *Manner & Customs of the Bible,* Whitaker House, Springdale, PA

Great People of the Bible and How They Lived, 1979, The Reader's Digest association, Pleasantville, NY

Keller, Werner, Ph.D., 1956, *The Bible as History,* William Morrow & Co., New York, NY

Lockyer, Herbert, 1967, *All the Women of the Bible,* Zondervan, Grand Rapids, MI

Morris, Henry, Ph.D., 2000, *Biblical Creationism,* Master Books, Green Forest, AR

The Cambridge Bible Commentary, 1979, Cambridge University Press, New York, NY

The Illustrated Family Encyclopedia of the Living Bible, 1962, San Francisco Productions, Inc., Chicago, IL

Woodmorappe, John, 2003, *Noah's Ark: A Feasibility Study,* Institute for Creation Research, Santee, CA

Vos, Howard F., 1990, *New Illustrated Bible Manner & Customs,* Thomas Nelson Publishers, Nashville, TN

A Final Note From the Author

Dear friend, are you ready to heed God's call for repentance? Are you ready to enter into the ark of salvation? Don't delay. NOW is the time to turn your life over to God, for He is merciful and forgiving. NOW is the time to accept Jesus Christ as your Lord and Savior! Wouldn't it be wonderful to sit at the feet of Noah and his faithful wife and listen to them tell the story of the flood as it actually happened? That experience can be yours in God's paradise made new!

Contact Information

For further information about this book you may contact Jean Holmes at <JeanHolmes@aol.com>.

Mary Margaret Buss, professional actress and author Jean Holmes, invite you to step into a world where art, history and theater intersect in the thrilling **Faith Forum** program. During their riveting exploration of this Old Testament story, Scripture takes on richer meaning as they open an intimate window into the life and times of the Family Noah.

Our time together will be a dynamic mix of elements that will help you understand the importance of the Great Flood and its relationship to end-time events:
- Dramatic portrayals of the story of Mrs. Noah
- Readings from *The Women of the Ark*
- Bible study workshop
- Creative writing
- Interactive exercises

Naamah, wife of Noah, beckons you to see the world through her eyes. For further information, concerning portrayals of Mrs. Noah or other women of the Bible including Mary Mother of Jesus, Ruth, Mary & Martha, Mary Magdeline, His Majesty & the Magi, & The Woman at the Well, contact Mary Margaret Buss at: www.mmoneshow.com

About the Author

Jean Holmes lives with her husband, two cats and one dog in Delray Beach, Florida. She is a free-lance writer who has authored some 300 fiction and non-fiction stories and articles ranging from subjects on nature and science to Bible studies and teacher's program helps. Jean has authored two children's books entitled *Norah's Ark* and *Sea Island Sanctuary*. Her five-book **Weldon Oaks Series** for young adults offers a thrilling account of the Gullah People of the Sea Islands of South Carolina and Georgia. These fictional though historically correct books take the reader from the period immediately prior to the Civil War through Reconstruction. The titles in this series include: *Mornin' Star Risin'*, *Deep River Lawd*, *'pon Jordan's Far Shore*, *Jubilation Morn'*, and *Bound for Glory*.